Lon Hieftje

I0685366

Jordan Kingston
Keeping the Secret

By Lon Hieftje

ISBN - 978-0-9982994-0-2

ISBN - 978-0-9982994-1-9 eBook

Dedication

I dedicate this book to my wife, Laurie, who is an avid reader and has put up with my endless hours in front of my Surface writing this book.

I also dedicate this book to my two grandsons, Jordan and Brayden, of whom I used their names as the main characters.

Preface

After finishing the first book Jordan Kingston and the Unknown, I saw the possibility of a sequel. Reading Jordan's first book is highly recommended to help you understand this continued story.

In Jordan Kingston Keeping the Secret, Jordan and his cousin, Brayden, will take you on a ride through the believable or unbelievable possibility of Aliens.

Are extraterrestrials spying on us? Did people see flying saucers? How about those crop circles? Have you ever thought there are aliens and flying saucers flying around making them? Or, are there just some pranksters out there having fun in the fields? What about Roswell, New Mexico? In July 1947, a craft crashed in the desert. The Roswell Army Airbase was involved in recovering the craft and there were, possibly, "bodies" reported?

Okay. Now, truthfully, what do you think?

Have you seen a UFO, or do you know of someone who swears they have seen one?

Jordan Kingston, the main character, along with his best friend (and cousin), Brayden, explore the possibilities that aliens visited earth thousands of years ago, and maybe even now. Jordan is a believer in "Alientology," a word coined to describe the study and belief in aliens and how they have impacted human civilization. Jordan believes in the possibility that extraterrestrials did visit the Earth in ancient times giving knowledge and guidance to ancient civilizations so as to advance their cultures.

There came a time when Jordan, and eventually Brayden, were introduced to real Aliens by their grandpa. They were brought into a group the Aliens call the "Knowing."

Jordan, now in the Knowing group, was taken aside and told that he is an Alien himself. Going through many learning sessions, he will be taught everything from the Aliens past to the present. Now Jordan is under Tarke's guidance, the captain of the Alien's spaceship at the bottom of Lake Michigan.

You have the book open, so get in and enjoy their continued journey through Jordan's adventure trying to find out as much as he can and keeping his secret.

The story continues . . .

It's been a long, interesting, fact finding, and challenging summer. Jordan has gone through many learning sessions with Tarke by his side. With summer slowly coming to an end, it's time for Tarke to take a long-deserved break.

"Good morning, Jordan," says Tarke, as he walks into the lunch room where Jordan is finishing breakfast.

"Good Morning, Tarke," Jordan replies, as he takes a sip of his juice.

Tarke picks out a breakfast drink and takes his seat at the table with Jordan. "I have been doing a lot of thinking lately, and it's time for you to take a little more responsibility." Tarke looks at Jordan. "I'm going to visit your grandfather for a couple of days."

Jordan looks up at Tarke. "That sounds like fun for you and Grandpa," he says with a smile.

"I have had you by my side and I'm very pleased with how you have handled everything," Tarke says, looking at Jordan. "This morning I'm going to make an announcement to the crew telling them that I'm going to take a couple of days off and you will be in command of the ship while I'm gone."

Jordan asks, "You think that I'm ready for this responsibility?"

"Yes, I have full confidence in your ability. You have handled every job that I have given you with ease," he tells

Jordan, as he finishes his breakfast drink and stands up. Jordan had finished his breakfast, so he gets up to walk out of the lunch room with Tarke. They go up to the main ship's control room where Tarke takes a seat in the captain's chair and with a wave of his hand over the control panel, he looks at Jordan, "attention team... I have an announcement. Attention team," he pauses, "I'm going to take a couple days' break starting today. I'm immediately placing Jordan in command of the ship for the next three days. With my full trust and your respect, here is your captain."

Tarke stands and motions Jordan to take the captain's seat. Jordan takes the captain's seat, looking around the control room as the workers are watching him.

"It's all yours for the next three days, Jordan. Take command and make your first announcement as commander."

Jordan waves his hand over the main control panel. "Thank you, Tarke, and everybody for your support. I'm anticipating a good time working with you and getting to know you more as we give Tarke a few enjoyable well deserved days off. Thank you."

Jordan waves his hand over the control panel turning it off and stands with Tarke.

They go back down to the central area of the ship as Tarke heads for his room to get his things ready for his visit with Jordan's grandparents.

Jordan sends a message to Pete, *"Pete, will you get Tarke's transporter ready for him, please."*

Pete responds, "*Yes, Captain, sir, I'm getting it ready now.*"

"*You don't have to call me Captain,*" Jordan replies.

Pete messages back. *"I'm just having fun with you; can't a brother do that?* "

Jordan messages back with a grin on his face, "*Okay, Bro, I can deal with it.*"

Jordan looks down the hallway and can see Tarke coming with a sports bag in hand.

As Tarke walks up, Jordan tells him, "Your transporter should be ready. I had Pete get it out for you."

"Thanks, you are on the ball. I knew you would be," Tarke answers, as he is walking to the bridge.

Pete comes walking out of the bridge corridor. "Your transporter is waiting for you. Have a pleasurable couple of days off, sir."

"Thanks," answers Tarke, as he walks into the bridge to the transporter.

Jordan and Pete stand there watching as Tarke leaves.

Pete looks at Jordan, "could you have ever thought that you would be in charge of a space ship? Or like Brayden would say, UFO."

"No, not in my wildest dreams," he answers with a smile. "Let's go to the leisure room and visit for a while." They head to the leisure room.

As they are on their way, Jordan is stopped by one of the crew, "Congratulations, Jordan, on your promotion," he says as he reaches out to shake his hand.

"Thank you very much for your support. May I ask your name?" Jordan asks as he reaches out to shake.

"I'm Scan," he answers.

"Now that's an unusual name. Scan....I like it." Jordan gives him a good shake of the hands.

Jordan and Pete enter the leisure room and take their seats.

"Well, Pete. This summer has been more than I could ever have begun to dream of. I'm now temporary captain of this ship, and I have a brother," looking at Pete and trying not to cry. "And, I'm actually one of those Aliens that I believed in so much. It's a wonder that I haven't fallen into the loony bin with everything that has happened."

Pete is looking at him with a big smile. "Jordan, you are too smart for the loony bin. In our society, each one of us is groomed for a particular job. Mine is transportation, and with your knowledge, your job is to be commander of a ship like this."

"Okay?" Jordan agrees with a question. "I have been told that they have plans for me."

"Yes, Jordan, I have known about you for a long time. The Elders have had your future planned from the beginning of your life." Pete looks around the room for a moment, "you have been a believer all your life, haven't you?"

"Yes, I have," he agrees.

"There are reasons for that. Look back when your grandfather first took you out on his boat to meet me," Pete says as he is looking at Jordan. "Yes, it was a shocking experience, but you got over it with the belief that it was true."

"Yes," agreeing with Pete. "It didn't take a lot of explaining; I believed Grandpa."

"Now put Brayden in your spot, being a non-believer," Pete tells Jordan.

Jordan thinks about it for a minute. "Oh yes," he says in agreement. "I got it. It would have been some elaborate joke to him."

"Yep, the Elders took their time with you and did their diligent planning."

"I'm happy they did; I don't think that I would have liked the loony bin," Jordan says with a smile. "It's been nice talking with you; it's time for me to do my job." They both get up, "Pete, I'm so happy to have you as my brother and can't wait to get to know you even more."

With a hug, they walk out the door.

Jordan walks over to the lift to go up to the main control room. There he takes his seat in the captain's chair. Jordan just sits there for a couple of minutes looking around and starts thinking; *I'm actually sitting in the captain's chair of a space ship. If Brayden was here right now, he would go crazy. Tarke is with Grandpa; he must be beaming with pride.* Jordan's thoughts go on for a while, then he snaps back to business as he waves his hand over the control panel and gets down to work.

Tarke Arrives

Tarke lands his Transporter in Jordan's grandparent's drive. He has it set on full invisible while opening the hatch. Upon exiting, he commands it to return to the main ship.

Tarke walks to the door and rings the bell. Grandpa had been waiting for him to arrive. It didn't take long for him to open the door. "Hi, Tarke, it's good to see you. How have you been?"

Tarke walks in the door, "I'm doing great, how about you and Shirley?"

"We are doing well, also. We are sitting out on the deck; let's go out there." They walk down to the lower level of the house and out on the deck where Jordan's grandmother is sitting.

"Hi, Shirley, it's nice to see you," says Tarke. She stands to greet Tarke, as he gives her a hug.

"Hi, Tarke, it's been a long time. Gordon told me that you were coming to visit for a few days."

"Thanks for giving me a place to stay," Tarke says as he takes a seat.

"You know that you are always welcome here," she says. She has known Tarke for many years, has always liked his foreign sounding name and thinks nothing more of it. Tarke has been a good friend. In the past, he would try to plan something special for them during his visits. This way

Tarke can enjoy his time off and experience earthly human living.

They sit back and take in the nice view of the lake as Shirley gives Tarke a glass of her homemade lemonade.

"Well, Tarke, do you have any big plans while you are here?" she asks, knowing that he usually does.

"No, not really, but I have been looking forward to going out on Gordon's cruiser sometime in the next few days. That would be fun."

"Yes, we can do that for sure," answers Gordon now knowing something is up, thinking, *Tarke can go on my boat any time he wants. He must have some other plans?* He knows Tarke will. "We can go for a cruise today if you want."

"You know that sounds good, let's go now. How about you, Shirley?" Tarke asks.

"No," she answers, "you two go; you probably have a lot to talk about. I'll stay here. No problem," she tells them not caring if she goes on the boat or not.

What Jordan and his grandfather don't know is that Tarke is there with business plans and on the vessel, he can disclose his business.

They talk, watching the people walking on the beach and the boats on the lake, as they sit on the porch finishing their lemonade.

Gordon and Tarke are out on Lake Michigan in the cabin cruiser. After a few minutes, Gordon slows the boat down and looks at Tarke, "okay what's up?" he asks.

"Why don't you shut the motor down and come back here so we can talk."

He shuts everything off and walks to the back of the boat and takes a seat. "So, what's up? It isn't anything with Jordan, is it?"

Tarke is looking at him, "it's everything to do with Jordan."

"No," he says looking at Tarke, "not bad, is it?" he asks.

"I have no problem with Jordan at all. I have Jordan as temporary captain of the ship right now," he says smiling at Gordon.

"That's great to hear! He must be doing something good," says Gordon with a feeling of relief.

"Jordan is a very smart young man, and I have all my trust and faith in him," says Tarke with a smile.

Tarke adjusts himself in his seat. "My problem is with Jordan's parents."

"Okay, what is the problem with them?" he asks.

"They expect Jordan to start college this fall and this is not needed. And most of all, that won't work with our plans for him." Tarke looking at Grandpa, "remember Jordan has had quite a few learning sessions and most likely has more knowledge in his brain than the college professors can teach him."

"So, what are your thoughts?" Gordon asks with a questioning look.

13

"I have talked to the Elders, and we agree that we have to bring them into the Knowing."

Gordon looks at Tarke. "Both of them?"

"Yes, Gordon, both of them. I'm thinking as soon as possible."

"I believe that we shouldn't go too fast. How about we work them into it for a while?" he looks at Tarke for a minute as he ponders that thought. "They are non-believers; let's take some time to come up with a good plan."

"Gordon, you are right. I have been working too hard training Jordan. We will work up a plan, so for the next couple days, I'm going to relax, think about it, and enjoy my time off."

"Tarke, how about I give you some manual labor? I'm going to let you captain the boat. You will have to actually steer it and manually control the speed," he says as he is looking at Tarke with a grin.

Tarke looks at the captain's seat, "manual?" he says with a smile as he walks over and sits down to take control.

With Grandpa sitting in the cabin by Tarke they go on a nice lake cruise.

"So, then Jordan is doing well. I'm so happy to hear from you how he is doing," says Gordon.

"Yes, Jordan is doing very well. That is partly why we need to bring his parents into the Knowing. He is going to spend a lot of time with us, and there will be no time or need for college." Tarke looks over at him, "how would he explain being gone all the time and not going to college?"

14

"Yes, that would be tough for him," he agrees.

"I hope that we can bring them in, in a way that they would be proud of Jordan as much as you and I are," says Tarke.

"Yes, I know them well. They will be proud, it's just getting them to understanding what has gone on behind their backs. Why weren't they told in the beginning, they will want to know," Gordon explains.

"Let me work on a plan; we'll get it worked out. I have some real crafty people on the ship that will help us come up with something," Tarke says with a grin.

"Why don't we head back to the marina? I know of a good place where we can get a good perch dinner."

Tarke asks, "will Shirley be coming along with us?"

"Why sure. I'll give her a call and tell her our plans." He makes the call to his wife.

After they dock the boat, they were off to pick her up, and then they go for a good meal.

Last day off

Jordan has been keeping up with his official duties and the crew has been fantastic to work with. When time allowed, he would contact Brayden for a short chat. It's going to be a camping night soon; they have a lot to talk about.

Tarke and Gordon are out on the beach walking the shoreline. "I have been doing a lot of thinking about Jordan's parents. I'm going to have a talk with Jordan about them."

Gordon answers, "That will be good."

Tarke looks over at Gordon, "I think that we will get him to start planting seeds about alien belief with them."

Gordon replies, "I would think that has been done with his years of reading and talking about his Alien beliefs."

"Yes, Gordon, you are right there," Tarke agrees. "I'm also thinking about using our portable information transmitter to help things along."

He looks at Tarke. "Okay, I got you now. I hadn't thought about using the transmitter," he agrees, "good idea."

"When the seeds are planted, maybe you can take them for a boat ride like you did with Jordan," Tarke says with a grin looking at Gordon.

They walk the beach, enjoying the lake and casual talk as they make their way back to the house. As they get close, they can see Shirley sitting on the deck enjoying the weather.

They walk to the deck, "hi, Guys; did you have a nice walk?" she asks.

Tarke takes a seat. "Yes, Shirley, we did. It's a beautiful day for a walk on the beach."

"Are you two hungry?" she asks.

Tarke looks at her, "thanks for letting me stay here. You don't have to make a meal; I have that covered. It's on me tonight."

Gordon replies, "again, Tarke?"

"Yes, again. Get ready; our ride will be here at 5 pm," he says with a smile.

It's now 5 o'clock and the doorbell rings; Gordon opens up the door. There stands a nicely dressed man in a suit.

"Good afternoon, sir. My name is John and I'm your driver for this evening."

"Hi, John, we will be out in a couple of minutes," he says as he looks outside to see a black limousine parked in the driveway.

"I'm in no hurry, sir; take your time," John tells him. "It's a beautiful day; I'll be waiting by the limousine," he says with a smile.

Gordon looks back in the house as Shirley and Tarke are walking towards the door.

Tarke is looking at the vehicle as they walk out of the house, "I see that our limousine is here."

Gordon replies, "yes, it is. This is our driver, John."

"Hi, Sir, you must be Tarke. I see in my itinerary that you have a good evening planned." John walks to the limousine and opens the door for them.

"Good afternoon, Ma'am," he says to Shirley as she gets in and takes her seat.

Tarke has Gordon enter the limousine next, then he enters and takes his place. John closes the door and then walks around and gets into the driver's seat. "Are we all ready?"

"Yes, John," answers Tarke.

Tarke had it all set up for a nice hour-long scenic ride south, following the lakeshore to a quaint little town where they have supper reservations.

Jordan is sitting in the leisure room as Karen walks in, "Hi, Jordan," she says as she takes a seat next to him.

"Hi, Karen," he says with a smile.

She looks at Jordan, "so this is your last day in command. How has it been?"

"Great; everybody has been so helpful and accommodating. It has been a good experience," he says as he is looking at her.

"So, what's on your mind today?" she asks.

Jordan looks around the room, then turns to her, "college, that's my question. What am I going to do?" he says with a questioning look.

"Yes," she agrees, "that is a dilemma," Karen says as she looks away thinking. "Tarke will be back tomorrow; I'm sure that he will help you."

"I can't be here, and in college at the same time, I have a big parent problem with this," he says, looking at Karen.

"I hadn't thought of that. You do have a problem." Karen is looking at Jordan, "say, have you talked to Brayden lately?"

"Yes, I have. We are going to camp out soon," Jordan says with a grin.

It was good that Karen changed the subject to Brayden and camping. They haven't been able to get together much in the last month, with all of his learning sessions and training with Tarke.

Karen looks at Jordan, "maybe I will drop by for a while when you two are camping, if that is all right with you?"

"Sure, that's okay with me, and I'm sure Brayden would be happy to see you."

"Great, it's a plan," says Karen with a smile.

Karen and Jordan had been talking and hadn't seen Pete walk into the room.

Pete walks up and puts his hand on Jordan's shoulder, "so camping, I have never camped. Is there room for your brother?" he asks with a big smile as he walks around the table.

"So you have been listening to us?" Jordan asks.

19

"Yes, I have been, and you two didn't know that I was here," he says as he takes a seat.

Karen looks at Jordan, "I've seen your tent, I'm sure you can squeeze one more person into it."

Jordan smiles looking at Pete, "you bet we can. I will make sure that you can have time off with Tarke."

They chuckle with Jordan's reply, knowing that he is now training for second in command of the ship. What he wants he most likely will get, in their thinking.

Tarke's Return

It's the last day of Jordan's command of the ship, and he is up early doing his duties trying to get ahead of everything for Tarke.

Jordan comes out of the lift from the main control room, and there stands Tarke. "Hi, Jordan, I see you are hard at work today."

"I thought that I would get ahead of things for you, and try to make your first day back a bit easier."

"Thanks, Jordan, that will be a big help. I do have a few things to catch up on today."

Jordan replies, "that's what I was thinking."

Tarke looks at Jordan with a smile, "I have heard nothing but good about you since I've been back."

"Everyone has been helpful and excellent to work with. Can we go to your office for a short talk?" asks Jordan.

Tarke looking at Jordan, "that is what I was thinking; let's go now."

They walk to Tarke's office and take seats.

"First, I want Harec and Karen here," says Tarke.

Tarke contacts Harec and Karen using his communicator.

"Jordan, I'm going to give you some well-deserved time off. Enjoy the rest of the summer, you and Brayden can get back to do your camping that you two enjoy."

Jordan replies, "that is some of what I wanted to talk to you about."

Karen and Harec walk into the room and take their seats.

Karen is looking across the table at Tarke, "by your smiling face, you must have had a good time with Gordon."

"Yes, we had a splendid time," Tarke answers; then turns to Jordan, "Jordan, I know that college has been eating up your thoughts."

"Yes," he agrees. "That is the other thing that I want to talk to you about," Jordan replies with a concerned look.

"This is why I have Karen and Harec here. Jordan, I had a conversation with your grandfather and we both agree." Tarke looking at Jordan, "your parents need to come into the Knowing."

"The Knowing? How can we do that?" Jordan asks.

Tarke looks at Harec, "you have the portable information transmitters. What do you think about using a transmitter to put, belief in us in Jordan's parent's brains?"

"We can do that easily, " answers Harec.

"Has this been approved by the Elders?" asks Karen.

"I have their okay," replies Tarke. "Harec, get a transmitter ready. Jordan, I want you to spend some extra time around your parents casually talking about your books about Aliens."

"I will get a transmitter programmed and ready. It will be nice for Jordan not to have to be so secretive," says Harec looking at Jordan.

Karen looks at Tarke, "I'll visit Jordan with the transmitter and apply the information to Jordan's parents.

I would like to meet both of them anyway." Then looking over to Jordan, "how about you set up a luncheon or supper date with them for us. That's when I will use the transmitter.

Tarke looks at them, "I'll leave it up to you two to come up with a plan to plant the needed beliefs," he says with a smile, knowing that the job is in capable hands.

Harec is looking at Karen. "I will get the transmitter ready; just give me a day to come up with the right information to use in the transmitter. I'll be in touch with you soon."

Jordan is looking at Tarke, "one more thing, Tarke, I would like to have Pete spend a night with Brayden and me for a camping weekend."

Tarke looks at Jordan, "we can arrange a couple days off for Pete. I don't believe that he has ever camped. That will be fun for him."

"Pete told me that it would be a first time for him. I appreciate your approval; it will be fun for us to spend time together."

"I can agree, Jordan; Pete has been waiting for years to be able to get to know you. Just give me a time, and I'll make sure that Pete has it off." Tarke looks around at the group, "is there anything else?"

Jordan looks at Karen and Harec, "I'm done, how about you two?"

Harec answers, "I'm good, how about you Karen?"

"I don't have anything more; I'll just wait for the transmitter, then for you Jordan to give me the go-ahead."

Jordan looks over at Tarke, "we have the plan, and now it's time for me to head back home. Thanks again, Tarke for your support. I'll now return home and get to work on my parents."

They all get out of their seats and walk out of Tarke's office.

Jordan messages his grandfather, *hi, Grandpa. I'm ready to go home. Do you have time to pick me up with your boat?*

Grandfather replies, *yes, Jordan, give me an hour. I'll message you when I'm in place.*

Jordan messages back, *thanks, I'll be waiting.*

Jordan walks around the ship and talks to a few of the crew members until he receives a message. *Hi, Jordan, I'm ready for you.*

Jordan replies, *thanks, I'll be on my way in a couple of minutes.*

Grandpa has his cruiser on Lake Michigan moving slowly north when Jordan's transporter surfaces alongside.

The transporter's hatch opens as Jordan rises, smiling.

"Hi, Grandpa," Jordan says, as he steps onto the boat.

Grandpa gives Jordan a quick hug, "Hi Jordan, Tarke had nothing but good to tell me about you when he was here. I'm so proud of you."

"Thank you, Grandpa. Tarke is a good man; he has helped me intensely."

Jordan sends the transporter back to the mother ship as Grandpa takes his seat at the controls of the boat and turns it around to head back to the marina.

"Grandpa... slow down and take your time; Tarke talked to me about my parents."

"So, what are your thoughts?" Grandpa asks.

"I believe that it's a good idea; it will make life easier for me," says Jordan.

"Yes, it will. Tarke messaged me with the plan a few minutes ago," says Grandpa.

Jordan looks at Grandpa, "Did he tell you about Pete?"

"No, what's up with Pete?"

"Pete is going to camp out with Brayden and me," Jordan says with a smile.

"That sounds like fun. I don't think Pete has ever camped before," Grandpa says as he guides the boat towards the channel.

"Pete told me that this would be his first time," Jordan says, knowing that his first-time camping will be fun for Pete.

Grandpa turns the boat into the channel heading to the marina.

The Plan

Grandpa drops Jordan off at home; he walks into the house to see his mother working in the kitchen.

"Hi, Mom."

Mother looks over at Jordan, "did you have fun staying on your grandfather's boat?"

"Yes, I did, they had a friend visit them for the weekend."

His mother asks, "so Grandfather didn't stay with you?"

"No, I had fun at the marina by myself, they have a nice little restaurant there and a lot of people to talk to," Jordan tells his mother, knowing that he won't have to lie to his parents about his whereabouts much longer.

"Well, I guess that's good that you don't mind being by yourself," she replies.

"I had a couple of my alien books to study. You should read one; they are interesting to read. I believe that they most likely have visited earth," Jordan tells his mother, trying to open a discussion about alien life.

"I think I'll leave the alien books to you. Your father might have read one. I believe that I did see him with one of your books once or twice," Mother tells Jordan, as she is putting dishes away in the kitchen cabinet.

Jordan is thinking, *I'm going to leave a book or two out in the living room; maybe they will read or, at least, look at them.* As he walks into his bedroom, Jordan's phone rings, "Hi, Jordan, are you home?" asks Brayden.

"Yes, I just got home."

"Good, I thought that I would get ahold of you the old-fashioned way," says Brayden.

"It is kind of nice to hear a phone ring. The other is suitable for private messages. What's up?" Jordan asks.

"I haven't seen you in a while. I would like to come over. Are you going to be home?" Brayden asks.

"Yes, come on over," answers Jordan.

"I'm on my way. See you soon," and Brayden hangs up the phone.

It didn't take long for Brayden to be at the door. "Hi Mom," he says to Jordan's mother, as he walks in the house.

"Hi, Brayden. Jordan is in his room," she answers.

Brayden heads to Jordan's room where he finds him going through his books and putting a few on his desk. "What are you doing?" Brayden says with a puzzled look.

Jordan looks at Brayden, "I'll tell you later. Help me find a couple of what you think are the best books."

"The one in your hand is good and I would say this one is a great one, also," Brayden says, as he gives the book to Jordan.

"Good, thanks. Let's go up to the camp."

Jordan takes the books out to the living room and puts them on the coffee table. Brayden is following him and wondering what Jordan is up to. They go out to the backyard to see Jordan's father cleaning his garden tractor.

"Hi, Uncle John," says Brayden.

"Hi, Brayden, what are you two up to today?" Dad asks.

Jordan is looking at his father, "we are going up to the campsite to check it out."

"Let's hook up the trailer and take a load of wood up to the campsite," Jordan's father says.

"That sounds like a good idea," answers Jordan.

Jordan's father hooks up the trailer and takes it over to the woodpile and they load it. With the trailer loaded, up the trail to the campsite they head. Jordan's father is driving the tractor with Jordan and Brayden walking behind it.

They arrive at the campsite and Dad pulls the trailer by the wood pile.

"When is your next campout going to be? You two haven't been up here camping much lately," says Jordan's father.

Jordan answers as he starts unloading the wood from the trailer. "Soon, hopefully in a couple of days. Brayden came over to talk about our next camping date."

"We were going to come up here to clean up the area, and talk about when our next camping time will be," Jordan tells his father.

"The area looks pretty good, and now you have enough wood for a few days of campfires," Father replies.

Jordan is looking at his father, thinking, *it's time we plant an alien seed.* "Brayden and I like to come up here and talk about our believing in Alien life. It's fun to sit here at night and look up at the stars and talk about them and are they out there, and are they here on earth."

"I have looked at your books when you leave them out. They are interesting and can make a person think about the possibility," Jordan's father answers. "Well, boys, I'm going to head back down to the house."

"Thanks, Dad, for helping us."

Jordan's father hops on his tractor and down the trail, he heads.

Jordan watches as his father leaves, then looks at Brayden. "Well, Brayden, do you have what I'm doing figured out?" he asks.

Brayden turns to Jordan with a questioning look, "I'm not sure. Are you going to have an Alien discussion with your parents?"

"You are on the right track; it's been decided that my parents are going to be brought into the Knowing," answers Jordan with a smile.

"Oh, okay." He pauses. "How are you going to do that?" Brayden asks.

"Unlike you, turning into a believer, my parents are not. So, my job is to get them thinking about Alien life, as you have seen me trying to do."

"Why do they have to know, and be brought in?" Brayden asks with a wondering look.

"I have to lie to them all the time about where I'm at; that's not okay. What is going to happen when I'm supposed to be in college?" Jordan says, as he is looking for a place to sit. "Let's go over and sit on our fallen tree. I have a lot to tell you."

They take their seats. They have used this fallen tree many times when coming up to the campsite and it's always been a good place to take a break and have a talk.

"Tarke has put me through a lot of training and, at this point, college is out of the question. With me spending a lot of time on the ship and with other jobs to come, it has been determined that it would be best if my parents come into the Knowing like you. That way I don't have to lie to them all the time like I have to do now."

"But they are not believers," Brayden replies.

"Yes, Brayden, they are not believers. This is where Harec and Karen come into play; they are going to convert my mother and father into believers," Jordan answers, as he is looking at Brayden.

Brayden looks back at the campsite, "oh yeah; how are they going to do that?"

"Well, I have been taught a lot of things through learning sessions by Harec on the ship. I know that you are a fast learner so give me time, and I will share what I can with you." Jordan stands for a minute to stretch. "We have information transmitters that can provide knowledge, ideas, and various information into people's brains. It's kind of like my learning sessions, only in a portable way." Jordan sits back down, looking at Brayden, "I say we because, as you know, I'm one of them."

"Yes, I know, but that doesn't change anything. You are still my cousin and best friend," Brayden replies.

Jordan reaches over and puts his hand on Brayden's shoulder, "you're my best friend, also, no matter what; let's never forget that!"

"So, you can put belief in Aliens in your parents' brains; that's cool," says Brayden smiling.

"Yes, so that is what we are going to do. We will need to get them warmed up by talking Alien life. Then Karen will plant the belief in Aliens in them with the portable transmitter."

"Cool, this is going to be fun to watch," says Brayden, as he stands.

Jordan also stands, "yes, it will be fun and scary at the same time if you know what I mean."

"I believe that everything will be good. Your people will help you with your parents' understanding," says Brayden, as he looks out at the camping area.

They go around the camp cleaning it up and getting the area ready for their next camp out. Jordan puts a hand full of small sticks in the fire pit and looks at Brayden. "I forgot to mention; Pete is going to camp with us."

Brayden looks over to Jordan, "that sounds like a good time."

"Good, I'm glad you agree. Let's plan on this Saturday," says Jordan.

They finish picking up the area and head back home.

Camp out

It's Thursday and Jordan messages Tarke. *Hi, Tarke, can you please give Pete this weekend off?*

Tarke replies, *your camping weekend, yes, I'll give him the time off.*

Thank you. Saturday and Sunday will work for us, Jordan answers.

I'll give Pete all the time you want. Message him and make your plans; have a good time, Tarke replies.

Jordan picks up his phone and gives Brayden a call.

Brayden answers, "Hi, Jordan."

"Camping this weekend is set," Jordan tells Brayden.

"Great, we are going to have fun. I'll be over around noon Saturday to help set up the camp," replies Brayden.

"See you Saturday," Jordan replies.

"Okay, bye," says Brayden and they hang up their phones.

For a week, Jordan has been talking Aliens and Alien life whenever his parents were around. Jordan now thinks that they will be happy to have him out of the house and up on the hill camping. He has been having fun with them, by probing them for their beliefs and ideas.

It's time to message Pete, *Hi, Pete; I'm sure that Tarke told you that you have the weekend off for camping.*

Pete replies, *yes, he has. I can't wait.*

Jordan responds with a message, *okay, be at the camp site at one o'clock. Brayden and I will be waiting for you.*

I'll be there; we are going to have fun! Pete replies and the messaging is over.

Jordan heads out to get all their camping equipment out and ready to take up to the camp. Life is a lot easier now that Jordan's father is allowing him to use his garden tractor and trailer to haul everything up to the camp site.

Brayden comes walking around the back of the house to see Jordan with the camping gear piled all over, on and around the picnic table. "You can't wait, can you?" he says, looking at everything.

"You got that right," looking at Brayden. "This is going to be a good time."

"I agree," says Brayden smiling.

"I told mom that there would be three of us, and we are going to camp out for two days," Jordan says, as he is checking to make sure that he has everything.

"I'm glad you have that covered. I brought over a cooler of drinks," says Brayden. "We better get started carrying all this stuff up."

"I have good news," Jordan says looking at Brayden. "Dad told me that I could use his tractor and trailer."

"What are we waiting for? Let's get it loaded then," Brayden says in anticipation of getting the camp set up.

It didn't take long for them to get everything up to the camp area with Jordan's father's tractor and trailer.

"I'm going to take the tractor back. Keep an eye open for Pete; he should be here any time now," Jordan tells Brayden as he gets on the tractor and heads back down the path.

Brayden starts getting everything arranged and in its place. He is taking the tent out of its bag and he hears a voice, "need some help?" asks Pete, as he steps out of the Explorer.

"Wow! You scared me; I didn't hear you land," Brayden says with a startled look.

"Yes, the Explorer is quiet," Pete says, as he turns and gives it the command to return to the main ship. "Where is Jordan?" he asks.

"He took his father's tractor back down to the house," Brayden says, as he finishes getting the tent out and ready to put up.

"Let me help you. I have never put up a tent," Pete says, as he is watching Brayden getting it ready.

"It's easy; it almost goes up by itself. I guess on your planet, all you have to do is push a button and pow a tent is up," Brayden says, looking at Pete with a joking smile.

Pete knows Brayden; he comes back. "No buttons, we just have to think setup, and bam its set up."

Brayden looks at Pete, "ya right, I half believe you." Then he looks at the tent equipment that he just unpacked, "one-half believes you; the other half says you are kidding me." He looks back at Pete smiling, "let's set this thing up before Jordan returns."

Both of them get down to business and set the tent up. As they are putting the sleeping bags in the tent, Jordan comes walking back into the camp.

"Hi, Pete, I thought that you would be here when I returned," he says, as Pete hands the last sleeping bag to Brayden in the tent.

The three of them work on getting the camp set up and everything in its place. Pete and Brayden take seats by the fire pit, as Jordan gets the fire started early in the day. They all figure, *what the heck we need a fire.*

"This is fun already, and I've only been here for a half hour," says Pete, as he watches Jordan working on getting the fire going.

Brayden looks at Pete, "I bet it won't take you long to find out why Jordan and I like our camping. When the fire is started, we sit back, and then our Alien talks start," he says with a grin.

"This is where we have discussed Aliens and life possibilities out there on other worlds. We have had some challenging talks here, haven't we, Brayden?" Jordan says, as he puts his last piece of wood on the fire.

Brayden smiling, "yes we have. I have had a very good time with my buddy Jordan. I have teased him every way that I could with his Alien beliefs."

"Yes, he sure did!" Jordan says looking at Brayden, "now what do you have to say?"

"I'm outnumbered here now," he says with a grin. "I have an Alien sitting next to me, and my cousin is an Alien, also, sitting on the other side of me. You got me." He falls out of his chair onto the ground lying there in defeat with a big smile.

"Okay, Brayden, you can get up. We have accepted you into the Knowing. You can consider yourself as one of us," says Pete, as he helps Brayden up and brushes him off.

"Oh, I'm more or less Alien? I'm an Alien to you," he says with a grin.

Jordan looks at Brayden and can't hold back, "more Alien than less," he says, as he sets his seat back up.

Pete sits back in his seat looking around at the camp, then at the fire. "Now this is nice; I can see why you like your camping. It's so peaceful here sitting by the fire. I could get used to this."

"No matter how complicated life can get, coming up here for a night of camping will put your mind at ease," says Jordan, as he uses a long stick to rearrange the logs in the fire pit.

"Well said, Jordan. I agree," says Brayden as he gets comfortable in his seat.

Jordan looks over at Pete and Brayden, "Karen stated that she would stop by for a while tonight."

Pete is smiling and says, "I talked to her and she has a surprise for both of you."

Brayden looks at Jordan, "you are the educated one after going through all those learning sessions. What can she surprise us with?"

"I don't know; I still have a lot more to learn. You know that you never stop learning," Jordan says with a questioning look.

Jordan, Brayden, and Pete receive a message from Tarke. *Don't look around; we have spotted a person behind you in the woods watching you.*

Jordan replies, *thanks for letting us know.*

We are watching him closely; I'll put Karen on him, replies Tarke.

All of a sudden, a person around Jordan's age comes walking out of the woods. They can hear footsteps and turn around to see someone that Jordan knows from school. It's Rick, not one of Jordan's favorite people. Rick is a know-it-all type of guy who always has something to say, whether you like it or not.

Jordan stands, "Hi Rick," he says, trying to be nice.

"Hi, Jordan, having a campout with the guys," Rick says with a smirk on his face.

Brayden replies quickly, "yes we are."

Jordan receives another message from Tarke. *We placed Karen in the woods where the person was first spotted.*

"So what brings you here?" asks Jordan.

Rick looks around and then at Pete, "Oh, I was just taking a walk in the dunes." He looks back over at Jordan. "I noticed that you guys are doing more than just camping."

Jordan looking at Rick, knowing that he is trouble and asks, "what do you mean by that?"

Rick is looking at Jordan with a grin. "I have been watching you guys for a while. Who is that guy or thing?" he points at Pete.

Pete thinks a message to Jordan and Tarke, *did he see me land the Explorer in the camp?*

"That's Pete! Who do you say he is?" Jordan asks, wondering if Rick did see the Explorer.

"I saw him come out of a flying saucer, and I have been listening to you guys talking. He says with a smile, "I got you guys. I'm going to make a lot of money when I tell the world what I found." Rick turns to walk away not knowing or wanting to find out what kind of powers that Pete might have, he just wants to get out of there fast.

"You don't have any proof. Who is going to believe you" says Brayden, as Rick is walking away.

Rick stops walking by a tree in the woods and bends down and picks up a bag and camera. "Here is my proof, Mister Brayden."

Brayden, Pete, and Jordan receive a message from Karen, *don't worry I took care of his camera.*

"Have fun, Rick; it's been nice talking to you," says Jordan, as Rick walks away.

Jordan receives a message from Tarke, *I like the way that you handled things, I have put Rick on our watch list. There won't be much that he can do without us knowing.*

Jordan looks at Pete and Brayden, "I just received a message from Tarke telling me that Rick is now on the watch list."

"He must have been laying down in the woods watching you two, set up the camp even before I arrived," says Jordan, as he is looking out in the woods where Rick came from.

"It's a wonder you didn't spot him before you landed?" questions Brayden.

"Yes, it's my fault. I should have scanned the area before I landed, I will from now on."

"We never see anyone up here, this is a first, but yes, we all will scan from now on," says Jordan.

"So, what is that surprise that you were talking about before we were interrupted by that Rick guy?" asks Brayden.

Pete looks at Brayden and Jordan. "Karen was here and helped us with our unexpected company."

Brayden looks at Jordan, "how did she get here to help and where did she go? You are the smart one."

"I don't know; I have a lot more to learn." Jordan turns to Pete, "my thought is, how did Karen come and leave is our surprise."

Pete smiles with his reply, "you are about to know." Pete sends a thought message to Karen, *it's time, by the tent as planned.*

Okay, Karen replies.

"Look over by the tent," Pete tells Jordan and Brayden.

They both stand in anticipation as they look over at the tent, knowing that something good is about to happen. All of a sudden, they see what looks like colored sand filling a mold. Slowly they see shoes forming, then up it fills to show legs. Then they can see shorts and, as the shape fills, there stands Karen with a smile.

Brayden looks at Jordan, "now that was cool! She teleported here."

Jordan smiles, looking at Karen, "I love your surprises."

Pete knows the TV and movies that Jordan likes to watch. He says, "yes, she beamed down," with a big smile.

Karen picks up a camping chair by the tent, walks over to the fire pit, and takes a seat with them.

Karen tells

Brayden, as usual, has his questions with their unexpected visit from Rick, and Karen's new arrival method. That has his brain full of thoughts. "Okay, Karen, your entry was cool. But my first thought is, our visitor that Rick guy." Brayden pauses for a second, "what did you do to help us?"

Brayden has Jordan's and Pete's attention, wanting to know what Karen will tell them.

Karen sits back in her seat, "when we spotted your observer, we saw that he had a camera and most likely had been taking pictures."

"He showed us his camera when he left," says Brayden with an angry look. "He thinks that he is smart, and is going to be famous with his pictures that he took."

Karen grins, "not so smart. He doesn't have anything on his camera, I formatted his memory card, and took a bunch of pictures of leaves and sticks on the ground with his camera."

"So he has nothing?" asks Jordan.

Karen answers, "yes, he has nothing put leaves and sticks."

Brayden smiles, "So he isn't going to be famous." Then he looks at Jordan, "you know him better than us. What do you think that he will do now after he sees his sticks?"

"Rick is a jerk and a self-centered person with few friends. He will be back with his camera." Jordan looks at Karen, "Tarke told me that Rick is on the must watch list."

Karen replies, "when he looks at his camera and finds the pictures that I took for him, maybe he will think twice about coming back."

"I doubt that" Jordan looks at Karen. "Rick will be back with a vengeance," answers Jordan.

"I have to agree with Jordan. I could see it in his eyes when he looked at me," Pete says in agreement.

"Hey, that's enough talk about icky Rickie, let's cook up some hot dogs," says Brayden, as he gets up and heads over to the food basket.

With Jordan's help getting everything ready, the hot dog roasting began. This was something new for Pete, and he kept asking everyone if they wanted another hot dog roasted. He was having fun and would have personally roasted them all.

Later after the hot dog roast, they are sitting around the campfire.

"How are you doing with your parents, Jordan?" Karen asks.

Jordan answers, "I think that I have planted enough seeds, if you know what I mean."

"Both of us have been working on them. The other day we had them in the living room watching alien videos," says Brayden.

"I'll talk to Tarke and Harec about using the transmitter soon," says Karen, as she gets up. "I think it's time to get back to the ship with my report."

"No, not yet," says Brayden. "You haven't told me how you did that beaming or transportation thing that you did when you came here."

Karen turns to Brayden, "I forgot, I know that you would never let me go without telling you how that works." She sits back down in her chair. "Transportation is something that we can do, but we don't use this option too often." She looks at Pete, "I'm not sure why I guess that we only use transportation in particular cases." She turns to Jordan, "transportation most likely will come up in one of your learning sessions."

"Will I be able to transport, also?" asks Brayden.

"That will be up to Tarke," says Karen looking at Brayden. "The transportation option is within your Medallion transmitter that you have. It has to be enabled for you to be able to use it."

"I know that I have to be serious about this. But it would be sweet!" says Brayden as he is looking at Jordan.

"Okay, guys, it's time for me to go," she says as she gets up and walks back a couple of steps. "I'll see you again soon."

This time, she fades out fast and is gone.

Brayden looks at Jordan, "this is just too cool, six months ago I would have never believed that I am looking forward to seeing Aliens and having them as friends of mine." He looks at Pete, "and now transporting from one place to another, like we just saw Karen do. And I have been in a UFO!" He sits back in his seat and looks up at the sky. "Wow."

Pete looking up at the stars turns to look at Brayden, "and I'm happy to have you as my Alien friend," he says with a big smile.

Rick looks

Rick quickly got back to his car after his surprise encounter with the group at Jordan's camp. With a smile on his face, he opens the door of his car and gets in. The first thing that is on his mind is to look at the photos that he took of the UFO and the Alien coming out of it. With a grin on his face, thinking, *I have something good here. I can't wait to show these pictures to the TV station; I'm going to make a name for myself. I have proof that Aliens exist.*

As he was walking through the woods taking pictures, he stumbled on Jordan and Brayden. Rick quickly lay on the ground hiding and watching them unload the tractor trailer of camping gear. As he was lying there, his devious mind was making plans on how he could disrupt their camping. He watched Jordan leave on the tractor and decided to watch Brayden. Then all of a sudden what did he see, a UFO appear in their camp! Seeing the UFO, he quickly started taking pictures of everything that he could, thinking that *wow, a UFO and an Alien.*

Sitting back in his car seat, he opens up his camera case and takes out his digital camera. With his anticipation running high he turns it on and goes to the view mode. He had taken quite a few pictures while walking through the woods; quickly he starts looking for his pictures of the UFO.

"Dang, what's up with this! Where are my photos?" Rick races back and forth through the pictures on his camera. Now looking through his camera and nothing could be found but sticks and leaves. "What the heck is this? I didn't take these pictures; I'm too good of a photographer to take this crap. Where are my good pictures, they are all gone!" He puts his camera in its case with a disgusted look, then starts his car and heads home.

Brayden, Pete, and Jordan spent the evening sitting around the campfire talking. Pete had to explain to Brayden how they camp on his planet. This became a fun discussion for Jordan to listen to, as he sat back in his seat watching Brayden and Pete go after each other. The conversation eventually changed to their visitor earlier in the evening.

"I bet that friend of yours isn't happy tonight," says Brayden to Jordan.

"Come on, Brayden; he isn't my friend. He never has been and never will be. I just wanted to be nice to him and not create any problems."

"Yes, I know. I'm sorry. I was just trying to make a joke," Brayden tells Jordan with a grin.

"Okay, you two... we all know, as I found out quickly, he is crafty and a different type of character," says Pete.

"That's true. He can be nice, but you have to be careful around him. I have talked to him a few times and he is smart, but he is always after what he can get out of you," Jordan explains as he puts another piece of wood on the fire. "I do promise you this; Rick will be back."

"Oh yes, I could see that in his eyes, when he was looking at me," answers Pete.

Brayden jumps out of his chair and runs over to the tent. "I'm getting my flashlight; you never know, he might be lurking around out there somewhere."

"Brayden get the light out of my bag instead, but do not turn it on," says Pete.

Brayden goes into the tent to get his flashlight and finds Pete's light. He comes out with his light and a small silver object?" "Is this your light?" he asks as he holds up what he thinks is Pete's light.

"Yes, that is it," Pete answers.

Brayden walks back from the tent and gives the light to Pete. "Okay Pete, show me why I shouldn't turn it on."

Pete takes his light, "this is not just an ordinary flashlight." Pete points it out to an area in the woods and turns it on.

Jordan looks at Brayden, "I know what this is, I know from my last learning session. This is going to be good. Show him, Pete."

Pete turns it on, "I told you not to turn it on because it is super high powered and can burn your eyes." The light is on with the brightness of a regular flashlight now. Then Pete adjusts the light, and the woods lights up just like the middle of the day."

"Now that is a flashlight!" Brayden says, as he looks back at Pete. "I need one of those."

"That light can adjust down to a small beam of light that can be seen from space," Jordan tells Brayden.

"A survival light. Cool," Brayden says as he is looking at Pete and his light. "If we suspect that someone is out in the woods, you can light up the whole area."

"Yes, I can. Remember, Tarke has this area on the watch list, and if Rick comes back they will know," says Pete, as he sits back down. "And if he is out there, I will light him up."

"Pete's right, Brayden, come on over here and sit down and enjoy the rest of the night by our fire."

Brayden takes his seat with his flashlight, looking at it thinking. *I need one of those survival lights; they are nice.*

They sit around the campfire until the early morning talking, before heading into the tent for a good night's sleep.

The next day

The sun is shining on the tent as they are waking up. Pete has been awake for a while, just lying there enjoying his camping time with Jordan and Brayden.

Jordan rolls over to see Pete laying there looking up at the top of the tent. "Good morning, Pete."

"Hey, I'm trying to sleep," Brayden says as he rolls over.

Jordan sends Pete a thought message. *Watch this.* "Mom and Dad told me that they would make breakfast for us this morning."

Brayden rolls back over and sits up, "breakfast?"

Jordan and Pete look at each other smiling, as they get out of their sleeping bags.

"Jordan I have been thinking this morning. What do you say that we get hold of Karen and Harec, then have her come to breakfast with the transmitter?" asks Pete. "I believe that Harec has the transmitter ready."

Jordan gets out of the tent and stands there a minute. "That is a good idea. I'll message Harec and Karen."

Pete exits the tent with Brayden behind him, as Jordan messages Harec. *Hi, Harec, do you have the transmitter ready for my parents?*

Harec messages back quickly. *Yes, I have it right here ready to make your parents believers.*

Great. Karen, are you there? *Yes, I have been listening.* Good, *are you free this morning?* asks Jordan.

Let me check with Tarke; I'll be back in touch with you in a couple minutes.

Jordan looks at Pete and Brayden, "the transmitter is ready, and Karen is checking with Tarke to get his approval."

"Can Karen use the transmitter at breakfast without them knowing?" asks Brayden.

Pete looks over at Brayden. "You bet she can. The transmitter will be programmed to search for Jordan's parents and deliver the information."

"I can't wait to see that happen," says Brayden with a big smile. "This is going to be too cool."

Jordan receives a message. *Jordan, Tarke says go! It's on, how do you want to do this?*

Jordan replies. *This morning, can you be here, or should I say at my house in a half hour?*

Karen sends her message back. *I'm calling the trolley now; I'll be there as soon as I can with the transmitter.*

Jordan looking at Pete and Brayden, "Karen is on her way. She will meet us down at the house, as soon as the trolley can get her there."

"I suppose that we should head down to your house then," says Pete.

"Yes, that's the plan. We can clean up before she arrives," Jordan answers.

"Yep, I'm hungry. By the way, do your parents know Pete is here?" asks Brayden.

"No, and yes. They have not met Pete, but they do know that we have a friend camping with us. For all they know, he came later in the evening."

They start down the path to Jordan's house and Brayden smiles as they are walking. "They will find out who Pete is soon."

They reach the house and they walk in the door. Jordan's father is sitting at the table with a cup of coffee. "Hi, Boys."

"Hi, Dad; this is Pete. Grandpa introduced him to me," says Jordan, knowing that Pete is a bit older than him and using Grandpa would help explain the age difference.

"Hi, Pete. It's nice to meet you." Dad looks over at Brayden, "hi Brayden, are you ready for breakfast?"

"You bet I am. We have another friend coming; I hope that this is okay," says Brayden.

Jordan's mother walks into the room, "Hi, Hon. This is Jordan's friend, Pete," says Jordan's father.

"Hi, Pete. Did you guys have fun camping last night? It was a beautiful evening," says Mother.

"Mom, Karen is coming for breakfast, also. She should be here any time now." Jordan looks at Pete and Brayden, "let's go and clean up."

Mother looks at them, "good idea; I'll keep an eye open for Karen."

They head down the hall where the bathroom is across from Jordan's room. Each one of them takes their turn cleaning up, then return to the kitchen. It was good timing. As they reach the room, Mother is opening the door for Karen.

"Hi, Karen," says Jordan. He looks at his father, "you haven't met our friend. This is Karen. Brayden and I met her at the beach."

"Hi, Karen; it's nice to meet you." Jordan's father looks over at his mother, "do you have things ready for breakfast?"

"Yes, everything is ready," she replies.

Jordan's dad stands up from his seat. "I was told that we would have company for breakfast today, so today I'm going to make pancakes for you."

"Pancakes sound good," says Brayden. "Is there anything that I can do to help?"

"Yes, thank you. You can take this out to the picnic table in the backyard." Mother hands Brayden a tray with dishes, silverware and cups. "I have everything else."

They all walk out to the backyard to see Jordan's father setting the hotplate on the grill, and Mother is spreading out a tablecloth. They take their seats at the picnic table as Brayden hands out the plates and silverware.

It doesn't take long; the grill is hot, and the pancakes are cooking.

Jordan, sitting at the table, messages Karen. *I take it that you have the transmitter ready.*

Karen looks at Jordan and nods her head in a yes motion and messages back. *I'll turn it on and deliver the information when your parents sit down.*

Jordan smiles back thinking to himself; *I can't wait to be able to be truthful to Mom and Dad.*

Karen messages back. *I heard that Jordan; it will make life easier for you.*

Jordan's mother has a big plate by the grill that Jordan's father is filling with pancakes. "Chow down, before these get cold," she says, as she puts the plate on the table. "Here they are, dig in."

"Don't be shy, guys. Take your pancakes; Dad is making more. Brayden and I can wait." Jordan gets up and makes sure that they take their share. He takes the plate over to his father and he fills it again.

"Come on, Dad. Take a seat and visit. I'll finish the last batch."

"No, I'll finish this batch and then I'll come and join in."

Jordan returns to his seat and puts the plate of pancakes down on the table.

"Dig in, they are good and going fast," says Brayden as he takes another pancake. "What do you think, Karen and Pete?"

"These are the best. Jordan, you haven't told me your parents' names."

"I'm sorry; my father's name is John, and my mom's name is Gloria," Jordan answers.

"It's nice to meet you, John; your making us breakfast is unexpected and very nice. Gloria, I have met you earlier and know you as Mother, it's been a pleasure."

"Boy that's nice but a bit mushy," Brayden says with a big smile.

"I agree with Karen with the only exception; this is my first-time meeting Jordan's mother. It's nice to meet you, Gloria," says Pete.

"Wow, thank you. I always knew that Jordan would have nice friends; he's a good boy," Mother replies.

Jordan's father walks over to the table and grabs the plate to put the last batch of pancakes on it.

"Good pancakes, John. Now it's your turn to sit down and enjoy them," says Pete.

They all are sitting at the picnic table enjoying their breakfast as Karen has the transmitter on and delivering its information. Jordan and Brayden keep watching them trying to see if they can see any difference in their behavior.

Message delivered

Karen messages Jordan and Pete. *We are done, the message has been installed.* She smiles at them.

Pete messages back. *I'm going to give their new belief a try.*

Pete, looking at Jordan's mother and father, "so Jordan is quite the Alien researcher and believer, isn't he?"

Jordan's father replies, "he sure is. His mother and I have been shown by our son that Aliens are most likely real and have been here, and I also believe they may be here now."

"Jordan has come up with quite a few reasons why we have to believe. I think that we both agree," Jordan's mother says as she is looking at Jordan's father.

Jordan is sitting at the picnic table feeling extremely happy and looks over at Brayden smiling. Brayden looks back with amazement on how the transmitter worked, thinking, *it didn't even touch them, and nobody has even seen it.*

"We have had some good talks about his beliefs," says Karen as she jumps into the conversation.

"Pete found that out last night up at our camp with our discussions about Alien life as we sat around the campfire," says Brayden, as he has an idea. He thinks a message to Jordan. *What do you think if we introduce them to you and the Aliens up at our camp?*

Jordan looks over at the path going up to the camp. He messages back. *That will work, but not now. We will talk about it later.* Brayden answers back. *Okay, we'll talk later. I'm going to help your mother clean up,* Jordan replies with a smile.

Brayden stands up from his seat, "I'm going to help you take the dishes into the house."

"You don't have to do that; I'll take care of them," Jordan's mother replies.

Brayden looks at Jordan's mother, "no, Mom, enjoy your company. I want to do it for you," and he starts picking things up to take into the house.

Karen starts to get up, "I'll help you."

"No, Karen. Enjoy your visit; I'll take care of this."

Karen sits back down, "that's sweet of you, Brayden. Thank you."

It didn't take long for Brayden to take care of everything and return to the table and join in on the conversation.

Jordan's father is looking at Brayden with a smile. "You forgot the grill."

"That's your son's job," Brayden answers, knowing that Jordan's dad is kidding him.

The talk goes on for an hour or so about Jordan and his belief in Aliens and then how Brayden would give Jordan a hard time about his Aliens while camping; to Brayden, dressing up like an Alien and making a visit with Jordan's mother that ended up with everyone in tears of laughter.

They are back up at the camp seated watching Jordan as he is getting the camp fire started.

Pete gets up to give Jordan a hand, "may I help?"

Jordan is kneeling down by the fire, "sure give me a couple of those small sticks."

Pete picks up a handful of sticks and hands them to Jordan. "What do you think about your parents and the Knowing?"

"I listened to them today and believe that they are ready. I can't make the final decision; that will be up to Tarke."

Karen jumps in, "I have already given my report to Tarke," she says, looking at Jordan. "Tarke told me that you could make the final decision; his trust is in you."

"How about up here at the camp, like I suggested to you in my message," asks Brayden.

"I think that is a good idea," says Pete.

Jordan finishes with the fire and stands up. "Let me think about it for a while." Jordan walks around and takes a seat.

"I'm in agreement, that's a good idea Brayden," says Karen.

Jordan thinks for a minute, "okay, here it will be." He looks at Karen and Pete. "I will have my grandfather involved, also; this will be the clincher." Jordan stands and looks around for a minute. "First, I have to get them up here."

"Brayden and I will do that; they won't be able to refuse our asking," says Karen with a little smile. "Let's try this afternoon?"

Jordan is walking around pondering their suggestions. Then he turns to them. "Here is the plan. I will contact Grandpa. Pete, I want you to pick him up with the Explorer. After Karen and Brayden have my parents up here, I will have a talk with them. Then when ready, you and Grandpa can land here and show yourselves in the Explorer."

Karen looks at Jordan, "this afternoon is the plan; how about Brayden and I go down and invite them up here for this evening? That will give them advance notice so they can plan on coming up here."

"Okay, figure seven o'clock, I will have you two go down a little before seven to walk up here with them."

They continue to make their plans for this evening. Jordan is happy and apprehensive at the same time, knowing that his parents' lives will make a significant change today.

Grandfather arrives

Karen and Brayden had gone down to invite Jordan's parents to a campfire this evening. Jordan's mother hasn't been up to their campsite in a couple of years and was looking forward to seeing it again. She is going to bring up some marshmallows for roasting over the campfire. Jordan's father thought that it was nice to be invited.

Jordan messages Tarke and Grandpa. *Hi, Tarke, my plans are to bring my parents into the Knowing this evening.* Tarke replies, *Karen says that they are ready, I will be watching everything.*

Jordan sends another message. *Thanks, Tarke, for your support. Grandpa, I want you to arrive at the campsite with Pete in the Explorer.*

Grandfather replies. *What time?*

Jordan answers. *Pete will pick you up around eight this evening; you can make your plans with Pete on where and how you will be picked up.*

Grandpa answers. *Okay, I'll contact Pete.*

With the plans made, Jordan takes his seat at the fire pit and leans back; then looks over at Pete, "this afternoon," he starts saying, with a questioning look.

"It will be good brother, it will be good," says Pete, knowing that Jordan has a lot on his mind.

Brayden speaks up, "let's take a walk to our favorite spot by the lake," trying to ease Jordan's thoughts about his parents.

"That sounds good, I've been there," Karen agrees, "and it's a beautiful place to relax. Come on let's go," says Karen, as she gets up from her seat.

Pete stands, "I'm ready; I want to see this beautiful place."

"Okay, let's go." says Jordan, "I do need to take a walk, and yes, Pete, it is a nice place overlooking the lake."

Brayden starts walking, "follow me I'll lead the way."

They head into the wooded area, where there is no path, but a nice easy walk through the hills towards the lake.

After a short fifteen-minute walk Brayden turns, "here we go, Pete. How's this for a view?"

Pete stands alongside Brayden looking out at Lake Michigan. "This is what you said it would be; a beautiful view."

They sit down in the sand on the top of the hill overlooking the beach.

Karen looks at Jordan. "I remember our meeting here when I grilled you about your Alien beliefs."

"Yes, you got on me about my beliefs pretty good that day," Jordan replies with a smile.

Pete nudges Jordan, "and remember the first time that we met on your grandfather's boat."

Brayden jumps in the remembering thoughts, "how about standing by the campfire and the Explorer pops up in front of me! I was shocked by what I was seeing."

Karen looks over at Jordan and Brayden. "Just think about it, the both of you handled everything just fine." Karen looks back out at the lake. "I don't want to be corny sounding; 1 hope that all of this has been a beautiful experience," then looks back at Jordan. "The both of you have handled your new knowledge very well."

"Yes, we have. It's been more than what I would have ever dreamed of," Jordan agrees.

"So think about it; Harec installed an Alien life belief program into the transmitter, and that information was given to your parents." She looks out at the lake again, "it's going to be a beautiful experience for your parents, also."

"Thanks for your help calming my thoughts, Karen. I'm thinking more positively about this evening." Jordan gives Karen a quick hug. "I think it's just the anticipation that got to me."

They now have Jordan calmed down, and the laughter starts with Brayden telling slightly enhanced stories of his questions and alien experiences before they head back to the camp.

After making hamburgers on the grill that Jordan set up over the fire for their supper, and enjoying a good meal; it's now time for Karen and Brayden to go down to get Jordan's parents.

They arrive at the house to see Jordan's father sitting at the picnic table.

61

"Hi, John," says Karen.

"Hi, Karen. Gloria is in the house filling her bag with goodies to take with us."

Brayden, looking at the back door, says "here she comes."

Jordan's father gets up from his seat and they head over to the path and up to the camp.

"We have a good fire going," says Brayden, not knowing what to say as they are walking. "Oh, I forgot. I need to get two more camping chairs."

"There are a few in the back of the garage. Do you want some help?" Jordan's father asks.

"No, I will get them. I'll catch up with you." Brayden heads back to the garage.

Jordan's mother is looking up the path, "this is going to be fun. It's been a long time since I have been up there."

Karen looks over at Jordan's parents as they are walking up the path. "I have only been at their camp a couple of times, and it's nice. Jordan told me that you made the fire pit and help him keep the wood pile full," Karen says, as she turns to look up the path.

Father replies, "both of us did a lot of clearing and made the area nice for setting up camp."

Karen turns to look back down the path, "I see Brayden coming."

"Brayden is a good boy," says Jordan's mother.

They stop and wait for him.

"Give me one of them," says Jordan's father, holding out his hand.

Brayden hands him one of the chairs and they head up to the campsite.

Jordan looks back at the path to see the four of them coming.

Pete can see two of them carrying chairs. He gets up and moves the chairs that they have around the fire pit, making room for two more.

"Wow, this is nice, Brayden," Mother says, as she is looking around. "I can see now why you two spend so much time up here."

"It is nice. Let's put your chairs down here; then you can take your seats and enjoy," Pete tells them, as he points to the open area that he made for them.

Brayden sets the chair in a place that he has, by the fire for Jordan's mother. "Here you go, Mom."

Mother hands her bag to Jordan, "I packed some things for us." Jordan takes the bag and puts it on the camp table.

"Thanks, Mom."

Jordan's father puts his chair down and they take seats around the fire.

It's around six o'clock, and the plan is that Pete will take a walk around seven, then teleport to the Explorer to pick up Jordan's grandfather. The meeting time will be determined by messaging.

They are enjoying the fire as Brayden thinks; *I'm going to start the Alien discussion.* Then he starts, "Jordan and I sit here every time that we camp and look up at the stars in the sky, wondering about Alien life out there."

Jordan's father speaks up, "I'm sure they are up there, but which star would be a good question."

Jordan suddenly receives a message. *Jordan, it's Tarke, you have someone coming your way.* Jordan replies. *Thanks, Tarke, no problem I'll keep my eyes open.*

Jordan looks at Pete and Karen. They nod their heads in an okay motion, hearing the message also.

Pete messages Jordan. *I'm going to get up and take a look.* Tarke sends Pete a message. *He is coming from the lake side of the campsite.*

Pete walks that way looking and can see Rick coming.

In the camp walks Rick with his camera. "Hi, Alien," he says as he walks into the camp.

Jordan's parents turn to Jordan with a questioning look.

Jordan stands, "Rick, what are you up to today?"

"I figured that your Alien friends erased the pictures in my camera and I'm going to capture new photos sooner or later," says Rick with a grin. "I see that you have a few more whatever you want to call them, sitting around your camp."

Jordan's father stands up, "who do you think you are? I'm Jordan's father, and I think that it would be best if you get the heck out of here before I remove you."

"Oh, you're Daddy. So, you aren't an Alien. I do know that guy is. I took pictures of him arriving in a UFO yesterday," Rick says, as he points at Pete.

Brayden stands, "Rick, you are full of it, where is your proof? You can go now; nobody here wants to see and listen to your garbage."

Rick turns as Jordan's father steps forward. "I'll be back; you can bet on that," and he heads back into the woods.

Pete looks at Rick, "I'll follow you out of here."

"Don't worry. Alien; I'm leaving." Rick continues walking out into the wooded area.

Pete messages Jordan. *I'm going to make sure that he is gone, then I'll pick up your grandfather.* At a short distance behind Rick, Pete follows him until he reaches his car.

"Rick looks back at Pete standing there watching him. "See you again soon, Alien," and he gets into the car and drives off.

Jordan's father sits back down in his chair. "What was that?"

Jordan answers, "Dad, that is Rick, he is a trouble maker. He has been that way all through school."

Karen messages Jordan. *Are we still on?*

Jordan messages back. *Yes, Pete is on his way to get Grandpa.*

Karen replies, *okay, I'll try to help smooth things out and get you started.*

Jordan gives Karen one last message before she starts. *Let me message Brayden to let him know what is going to happen first.* He messages Brayden to let him know what is going to happen. *Brayden, Karen is going to get things started, please just sit back and let us handle this.*

Brayden nods his head. *Okay, Karen, go ahead and get started.*

Jordan's father is concerned with what happened, and wondering about them coming up here to camp anymore.

Karen, looking at Jordan's parents, "don't worry about camping up here; everything is under control."

Jordan's mother speaks up, "under control? How can you say that? That Rick guy seems like some kind of nut."

"I go along with that," says Jordan's father.

"Yes, he is his own person that's for sure," replies Jordan.

Karen looks at Jordan, "I can agree with that." She looks back at Jordan's parents. "Let's change the subject back to Aliens." She has their full attention, "Aliens are just like you and I."

"Okay, where are you going with that statement?" Jordan's father looks at Karen, "that Rick fellow brought up Aliens?" he questions.

"Well, actually yes he did, and that's our problem," answers Karen.

Jordan's mother is sitting there with her mouth open staring at Karen, after hearing what Karen just said.

Jordan's father stands from his seat. "What, Rick pointed at Pete, calling him an Alien!"

Jordan stands, "relax, Dad, and have a seat. Karen, I'll take over from here," and the both of them sit down. "Mom and Dad, Aliens are real and are here on Earth."

"Come on, son, I believe that they exist; but here?" asks Jordan's father.

"Yes, Mom and Dad, you are sitting alongside an Alien. Karen is not from Earth."

Jordan's mother and father both look at Karen.

66

Karen smiles, "Yes, I'm from another world."

Jordan's dad stands up again, "this is too much."

Jordan looks over at Brayden, "we are telling them the truth, aren't we Brayden?"

"Yes," he answers.

"I think that it is time to show them. Mom and Dad, come with me and let's stand by my tent. Brayden, will you move the chairs, please."

They walk over by the tent. Now Jordan's parents are entirely puzzled with what is happening. Brayden moves the chairs then walks over and stands with them by the tent.

"First, I have to tell you this; what you are about to see, you must never tell anyone. Brayden and I have known this, and could not even tell you. It will be your secret forever. Will you keep this secret?" Jordan asks his parents with a serious look on his face.

Jordan's parents are standing there looking at each other. "Okay, Jordan, it will be our secret," they answer with questioning thoughts.

Jordan reaches for the medallion from around his neck. "Dad, this is a transmitter that I can use to call the Alien ship."

Mother looks at Jordan, "your grandfather gave you that."

"Well, yes and no. We will get into that later. I'm going to call the ship." Jordan looks at the medallion and thinks a message. *Pete, do you have Grandpa?* He gets a reply. *Yes, we are right above you.*

Jordan looks at his parents with a smile, knowing what is about to happen. "Mom and Dad, look at the campfire."

They are watching the campfire with puzzled looks on their faces. Jordan messages Pete. *Come on down and stay invisible, I'll tell you when to show the Explorer.*

They are watching the campfire as it suddenly goes out. They look at their son Jordan with a questioning look.

Jordan is smiling, "watch the fire pit." He messages Pete. *Show yourself Pete.*

The Explorer comes into view. Jordan's parents are now holding hands as they see the Explorer. The hatch opens and who do they see?

"Gordon!" Jordan's father blurts out.

Grandfather walks out of the Explorer with Pete following him.

Jordan's mother is standing there quietly, trying to understand what she is seeing, thinking, that's my father; now letting Jordan's father ask the questions.

Jordan's grandfather walks up to his parents, "I think that we should have a seat and talk." He turns to Pete, "you can send the Explorer back now, Pete."

They stand there watching as the Explorer fades out of sight.

"Yes, Dad, Aliens are real, as you can see. Brayden and I found this out earlier this summer." He picks up a camping chair that they had brought up just for Grandfather. "Brayden has the chairs set up by the campfire; let's go over there and take a seat. We have a lot to talk about."

Jordan's parents walk back to their seats with Grandfather and sit down.

Jordan's dad looks at Grandfather, "Gordon, how long have you been keeping this secret?"

"Let's see, how old is Jordan?" He pauses for a second." I would guess around twenty-five years now; it's been awhile. I was introduced to what they call the Knowing, by the now captain of the main ship." Grandpa looks at Jordan's parents, "the hardest part of knowing is keeping it secret from everybody, even my wife."

"You mean to tell us that Mother doesn't know?" Jordan's mother asks.

"I have had to keep the secret from even her." Jordan's grandfather stands up in front of Jordan's parents. "I have to get serious, with what you have seen today; and now that you know that Aliens or extraterrestrials are here." He looks over at Karen and Pete, then back to Jordan's parents, "You have to promise that you two will never tell anyone about this and what you are about to know."

Jordan's father looks at Gordon and asks, "You mean there is more?"

"Yes, a lot more! We had Jordan and Brayden make the same promise, so please don't be upset with them." Grandfather looks at Jordan's parents seriously, "I need both of you to promise to keep the secret."

Jordan's father can see the serious look on Gordon's face. "Yes, I will keep this secret."

Mother is looking at Gordon. "What about Shirley? I will have to keep it secret from her, also?"

"Yes, you do! Jordan had to keep the secret from the both of you. Do you promise to keep the secret?"

"Okay, yes, I will; knowing that Jordan kept it from us."

Grandfather steps back, "I have to tell you this, if you let the secret out to anyone, I can't say what could happen to you or who you told the secret to. That is out of my hands."

"We understand, Gordon; we won't let it out," Jordan's father replies. "Now, Jordan, what have you two been up to?" he asks, as he is feeling better and now has questions that need to be answered.

Jordan tells

They are all sitting around the campfire looking forward to some good conversation. Jordan's parents have a lot of questions, and the rest of them are ready to jump in with answers.

Jordan looks at his grandfather, "I don't know where to start."

"I'll help," Brayden says as he turns to Jordan's parents. "As you know, Jordan and I love coming up here to camp, and Jordan always would bring up his belief in Alien life."

"Yes, as you are aware, it's been in my thoughts all my life," says Jordan.

"Yeah, I tried my best to give him a hard time and discredit his belief, with no luck," Brayden comes back.

"He sure did; he tried his hardest," Jordan agrees. "One day, Grandfather gave me a call and wanted me to go out on his boat. That is when he introduced me to Pete," says Jordan, as he looks over to Pete.

Pete jumps in the conversation. "Like today for you, it was quite a surprise. Jordan had to sit down and think about it for a while."

Jordan's father looks at Pete and asks, "You didn't land on Gordon's boat with that craft that you landed here with, did you?"

"No, I used the Transporter," Pete answers.

71

Jordan's father is looking at Pete with a questioning look. "Transporter?"

"The Transporter is what we use for underwater transportation. We haven't told you yet; the main ship is underwater in Lake Michigan."

Jordan's father looks at Jordan's mother. "This is getting good," and he turns back to hear more.

"Both of us have been on the mother ship, a real UFO," Brayden says with a big smile. "Jordan knew about the Aliens and the main ship, a while before they even let me know about them."

Gordon looks at Jordan's dad, "I had a talk with them on the main ship about bringing Brayden into the Knowing, simply because it was too hard on Jordan to keep the secret from you two and Brayden."

"So it was easier to keep the secret from us?" Jordan's father asks.

"No, Dad, it was very hard for me," answers Jordan in response to his father's question.

"Now, for good reason, it is time to bring you two into the Knowing," says Karen.

Jordan's dad looks at Karen, "so, what is your reason?"

Karen looks over at Jordan's grandfather. "I think that this is a question for you to answer."

"Okay, this is going to take some time. How about we get those marshmallows out and something to drink?"

Jordan's mother gets up from her chair, "that sounds good to me. We need to relax and enjoy the campfire this evening." She walks over to get her bag of goodies.

72

Karen gets up, also. "I'll help you. Jordan, where are the drinks?"

"They are in the cooler under the camp table by Mother. Brayden, you will have to get the roasting sticks."

They take a break from their discussions to enjoy roasting marshmallows. Jordan's father talked to Grandfather and Pete about the campsite, and how he loved camping when he was a kid. Karen had a nice conversation with Jordan's mother about her favorite subject, Jordan.

"Okay, Gordon, let's get back to why we are being brought into what you call the Knowing," says Jordan's father.

Grandfather sits back in his seat, "I guess that I will have to start way back eighteen years ago. Remember when we had the talk about adoption?" he looks at Jordan's parents. "It was something that you two had discussed many times. When you were shown Jordan, it was love at first sight and you wanted to accept him as your son. In a short time, Jordan was yours, and you had your long-wanted son."

"Yes, adopting Jordan was a dream come true," says Jordan's mother.

"You have me thinking," says Jordan's father, as he looks at Jordan.

"Yes, your thoughts are right. Jordan is an Alien clone; this is why he has that deep desire to know all he can about Aliens."

Mother looks at Jordan. "My son, Jordan?"

"Yes, Gloria, your son is an Alien clone. This does not, and should not, change your love for each other."

"Mom and Dad, I love you and I always will," says Jordan with teary eyes.

"John and Gloria, it was decided that it is now time that you would be brought into the Knowing. Gordon, can I jump in at this point?" asks Karen.

"Go ahead, Karen," Grandfather replies.

Karen starts, "this is all new and a lot to absorb this afternoon. I have to tell you this; you have a son that you can be very proud of. I will talk to Tarke, the commander of our ship, and make arrangements to show you our ship and meet Tarke.

"I would like to see your ship; I can only imagine what it may be like," Jordan's father says, as he looks at Jordan's mother. "What do you think?"

"I don't know; it sounds a bit scary to me," she replies.

"Mom, there is nothing to be scared about; everyone on the ship is very nice. You will like it," says Jordan with a smile, knowing that his life is about to get a lot easier with his parents now in the knowing; and he doesn't have to keep his activities secret from them.

The day after

It's early morning and Pete is getting ready to go back to the main ship. Jordan and Brayden are picking up around the camp and getting things ready to take back down to Jordan's house.

"I had a good time camping. I definitely want to do this again," says Pete. "I should head back in a few minutes."

"Go ahead; Brayden and I will take care of the camp."

"Good. I'll summon the Explorer to pick me up."

Brayden looks over at the path, "I think I can hear your dad's tractor."

They all look and here comes Jordan's father with his tractor and trailer.

Brayden turns to Jordan, "good, I didn't want to carry everything down. We have a lot of extra equipment."

Jordan's dad arrives at the campsite, "Hi guys, I got up and thought that you would like some help taking the camp equipment down," says Jordan's father with a smile.

"Thanks, Dad," says Jordan.

Pete looks at Jordan, thinking a message. *The Explorer is here. Now we can show the Explorer as your father is here. This is going to be nice.* And Pete smiles.

"Dad, Pete has to go. Take a look at the fire pit." The Explorer comes into view.

Pete walks over to Jordan's father and offers to shake his hand. "It was nice to meet you. We will definitely meet up again," and they shake hands. "It's time for me to go." Pete walks into the Explorer and the hatch closes, as the Explorer fades out of view.

Jordan's father looks at Brayden and Jordan. "It is going to take me a little while to get used to this."

"Grandpa first introduced me to them, and I had a few sleepless nights thinking about it," says Jordan.

"Me, too. It's not within our normal everyday thinking," Brayden says with a smile.

"Your mother didn't sleep much last night. Everything is still hard for her to digest. You will most likely be asked a lot of questions."

Jordan smiles and looks at Brayden. "Questions... what do you think this guy did when he was first introduced to them?"

Brayden just stands there with a smile.

"Let's get this trailer loaded," says Father.

A couple of full trailer trips down and the camp was clean and ready for the next time.

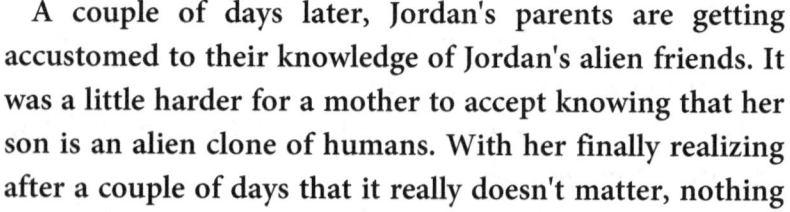

A couple of days later, Jordan's parents are getting accustomed to their knowledge of Jordan's alien friends. It was a little harder for a mother to accept knowing that her son is an alien clone of humans. With her finally realizing after a couple of days that it really doesn't matter, nothing has changed. Jordan is still her boy. Jordan has spent a day on the main ship with Tarke training and discussing his parents now in the Knowing.

"How are they going to be tested to see if they can keep the secret," Jordan asks Tarke.

Tarke answers, "when Harec installed the believing in aliens' program in the transmitter. He also added a program that instructed them to keep any belief and knowledge of them secret, and in the back of their minds."

"Why wasn't that done with Brayden and me?" he asks.

"We could have, but with your parents, that was an unusual case." Tarke grins, "besides that, I wanted you to meet Karen, and that was a fun way."

"So, you had fun with Brayden, also," Jordan says with a smile.

Tarke chuckles, "Brayden is fun to be around. He is almost too smart for me,"

"Has Karen talked to you about bringing my parents here?"

"Yes, there was a mention of them the other day, but we didn't get into it," Tarke answers. "Do you want to set up a time?"

"My father works, and I will have to have a talk with them to find out when a good time would be."

"Okay, Jordan, you have a talk with them and let me know," says Tarke. "By the way, I had a good conversation with Pete. He sure had a good time camping. I'm sure you will be asked about another date."

Another plan

Rick has been deep into trying to figure out how the pictures on his camera were erased. He knows that the aliens are superior beings, but he feels that he is smart enough to get around them. I will find a way to get my pictures is at the top of his thoughts.

He has been going through all the electronic and sporting stores for ideas. Rick will get his photos no matter what it costs. After days of shopping and nights of planning, he is now ready, thinking. *I'm going to get that goody two shoes Jordan and his alien friends. That UFO is mine!*

Jordan has a talk with his parents to determine a good time that they can break away to see the main ship. The plan is Friday afternoon.

Jordan sends a message to Tarke. *I would like to have my parents visit on Friday. Could you send Pete to my campsite to pick us up?*

Jordan receives a message back. *Hi, Jordan, Friday is good. Pete is on assignment Friday though. You can use your Explorer to transport your parents here to the ship.* Jordan replies. *That would be special; I don't even drive a car. My parents will be shocked.* Tarke sends a message back. *I can send Harec instead of Pete.* Jordan comes back.

No Tarke, I'll do it, How about one o'clock in the afternoon Friday? Tarke replies. *Sounds good. I'll see you Friday.*

Jordan walks into the living room where his parents are watching TV. "I just talked to Tarke and the plan is to be at the main ship at one o'clock Friday afternoon,"

"How are we going to get there?" Father asks.

"We have to be at the campsite at noon Friday," Jordan tells them with a plan for the extra time.

Jordan can hear his phone ringing, "it's my phone." He rushes back to his room. It stops ringing as he picks it up. Looking at it, he can see that it was Brayden. Jordan calls him back. "Hi, Brayden; you called."

"Yeah, what have you been up to lately?" asks Brayden.

"Not much; I spent a day on the ship with Tarke and made plans to take my parents there on Friday."

"Friday - can I come along?" Brayden asks.

Jordan thinks about it for a minute, "yes, we have room for you; you can go with us."

Brayden answers, "Great! I haven't been on the ship in a while."

"Brayden, remember that this trip is mainly for my parents."

"I know. I'll just tag along for the ride."

"Okay; be here no later than eleven-thirty in the morning, Friday," Jordan tells him.

"I won't be late; I can't wait. I'll see you Friday," says Brayden as he hangs up the phone.

Jordan walks back to the living room and takes a seat. Looking at Dad with a grin, "how do you think we are going to get to the main ship?" he asks.

Jordan's father smiles back, "in that flying saucer thing that your grandfather arrived at the camp in."

"Yes, you are right," Jordan says, knowing that he will have another big surprise for them.

"I don't know about this; I have never even flown in an airplane," Jordan's mother tells him.

"You will be okay, Mom, it's really a lot nicer than even your car. Besides that, the Explorer has an automatic anti-crash and guidance system."

"It sounds like you know a lot about them. You probably have been in one a few times," Father replies with a smile.

"Yes, Dad, more than you know. We will get into that Friday." Jordan gets up, "I'm going to go out and cut the grass.

Dad looks over at Jordan, "Good, it needs cutting,"

It's Friday, and the anticipation and suspense are high in the house. Jordan's mother has been pacing around the house like a caged cat. Jordan's father has been out cleaning up the garage, just trying to keep busy. While Jordan is having fun watching them, knowing that this is going to be a good time for them. Jordan has messaged Tarke early in the morning telling him about the excitement that is looming.

The side door opens and in walks Brayden. Jordan's mother greets him as she is dusting off the cabinets in the kitchen.

"Hi, Mom, where is Jordan?" he asks.

"I think he is in his room," she answers.

Brayden walks to Jordan's room to find him just sitting there. "What are you thinking about?"

"Have you seen those two? They are going nuts today," Jordan says, as he looks at Brayden with a big smile.

"I see that your dad is in the garage and your mother is cleaning up in the kitchen."

"That has been going on since six this morning," he says, as he is starting to laugh. "I think it's about time to head up to the camp. Let's get them ready to go," Jordan says, as he stands. "I need to go and clean up; then we can go."

"Okay, I'll start getting Mom and Dad ready," Brayden says, as he heads down the hall to the kitchen.

It didn't take long and they are on their way up to the camp. Mother looks over to Brayden, "what do you think about riding in that saucer thing?"

"You are going to like it, it's fun," Brayden answers.

Brayden starts to think, *there are four of us and the Explorer only holds four.* He instantly receives a message. *Brayden, I just heard what you are thinking. I'm going to fly the Explorer. Don't tell them; it's a surprise.* Brayden smiles as they are walking.

They reach the campsite and Jordan messages Tarke. *Hi, Tarke, I would like you to have a scan of the camp area to make sure it's clear for the Explorer to land.* Tarke answers,

I'm on it; they are scanning now. Jordan waits a minute then receives a message. *It's all clear; there is nobody around the area.* Jordan replies, *Thanks, Tarke. I have my parents here. I'm going to take them for a ride before we come to the ship for our meeting.* Tarke answers, *I'll see you in a few.*

Jordan looks at his parents, "are you ready?"

Jordan's father replies, "yes, Son, we are more than ready."

"Okay, Dad, I just called the Explorer and it will be here in a couple of minutes." Jordan looks at Brayden with a smile.

"This is going to be cool, Mom; you will like it," says Brayden, as he is looking at Jordan's parents.

Jordan steps forward; it's here. The Explorer slowly comes into view and the hatch opens.

Jordan looks at his mother and father, "follow me."

They walk to the Explorer with the hatch open to see that there is no pilot.

"Jordan, you didn't tell us that this is self-controlled," Jordan's father says, as he is looking in.

"Dad, let's get in and take our seats. Brayden, why don't you take the first seat."

Brayden enters first, then Jordan enters and takes his place. "Come on in. Dad takes his place as Mother has the last seat." They are all in and seated.

Jordan's father looks where Jordan is sitting. Jordan pushes the button to close the hatch, then moves the visibility slider down. "Dad, I was keeping this a secret.

This is my Explorer and I will be your pilot today," he turns with a smile looking at his parents.

"Jordan, you are going to fly this thing?" Mother says with a panic look on her face.

Brayden can't help himself, "Mom, look outside."

Jordan's parents look out to see that they are above the trees and can see Lake Michigan.

"Yes, Mom and Dad, I'm a trained pilot of this ship. Now let's take a ride."

Jordan's father is smiling with pride, watching his son in control of a flying craft. "This is your, what do you call it, Explorer?"

"Yes, Dad this Explorer is mine... we will get into more later when I show you the main ship."

"You show us? What about this Tarke fellow, the captain of the ship?" Dad asks.

Jordan looks over to his father, "we will get into that later. How about we enjoy the ride."

Brayden jumps in to help Jordan by changing the subject, "what is neat is that nobody can see or hear us."

"I hadn't thought about that," Jordan's father replies. Jordan looks at his map and sets a destination. "Here we go, Dad; I'm going to show you the capability of this craft." He steps up the speed as they head north.

Jordan's father is looking out the dome and watching the Michigan shoreline zoom by. "We are really moving!" he says.

"We have made it to the bridge in around four to five minutes," says Brayden with a big smile.

They slow down to view the big bridge. After viewing the bridge, Jordan picks up the speed and heads north a little further.

Jordan slows down as he makes a turn and lowers his altitude. "Mom and Dad, look out to your right."

They look out to see the Pictured Rocks Lake Shore along Lake Superior.

Jordan's mother is speechless with what she is seeing.

"Here you go, Mom, this is what you have been waiting to see, Pictured Rocks," says Jordan as he slows the Explorer way down, so they can enjoy the view.

"This is beautiful, Jordan. Thank you for remembering that I wanted to see this," Mother says, as she is looking at the sights.

They tour the area; then Jordan takes the Explorer up and heads back towards the main ship.

The tour

Jordan slowly sinks into the Lake Michigan water.

"We must be close to the ship?" says Jordan's father in a questioning mode.

"Yes, Dad, watch ahead of us."

The main ship slowly comes into view. "I see it," Jordan's father says showing some excitement.

They pull up to the ships bridge and stop with the hatch opening.

"Mom and Dad, you can step out now; I'll be right behind you."

They exit the Explorer and stand there waiting for Brayden and Jordan.

Jordan comes out and his father pats him on the back. "I'm proud of you; you really impressed me with your flying skills."

Jordan's mother reaches for Jordan's hand, wanting him to walk with her as they go into the ship. They walk into the ship's main corridor to see Tarke standing there waiting for them.

"Mother, Dad, this is Tarke."

"It's nice to meet you Mr. and Mrs. Kingston," says Tarke. "Jordan, what are your thoughts?"

"Let's go to the conference room first, so we can fill my parents in a little more on how I'm involved," says Jordan.

Brayden looks at Jordan. "If it's okay, I'll go to the leisure room and talk with some of the crew."

Jordan turns to Brayden, "that's okay; go ahead."

Jordan's father picks up on Jordan's response to Brayden, thinking *who is in charge here? Why didn't he ask Tarke? He is the captain.*

They walk to the conference room and go in to see Grandfather sitting there.

Jordan's father is looking surprised, "Hi, Gordon. How did you get here?"

"I came on the Transporter."

"Transporter? Okay, I give up, I'm just going to sit down and let you guys explain all of this to us," Jordan's father says, as he takes a seat.

Jordan is still holding his mother's hand and walks her to the seat next to his father. Jordan walks around by Grandfather and takes a seat.

Tarke takes his place at the end of the table. "Where do you want to start, Jordan?"

"Tarke, we went through a lot at my camp after bringing them into the Knowing." Jordan looks at Grandfather for his agreement. "I would like you to explain to them where you and I stand."

Tarke looks at Jordan's parents. "May I call you by your names?"

"Yes, I'm John, and this is Jordan's mother, Gloria."

Tarke jumps in, "Thanks, John and Gloria. Your son Jordan, as you know, is a human clone. Jordan was cloned for one reason, and that is to eventually be the captain of his own ship like this one."

Jordan's father looks at Jordan.

Tarke continues, "our youth in many cases grow up with a definite plan for their future. Why and how, you may be thinking. Our Elders keep track of positions like mine and know when new young blood will be needed. This is where Jordan falls into the picture. How can we do this you ask? We have learning sessions; this is where we can install a lot of information and knowledge into a person's brain quickly. Jordan has been going through many learning sessions. The Elders came here from our planet to meet your son and promoted Jordan to be my student for second in command of this ship."

Jordan's mother and father look at Jordan with pride on their faces, with nothing they can say, wanting to hear more of what Tarke has to tell them.

Tarke continues, "I have taken time off to stay with Gordon and put Jordan in command of this ship and I will do it again. Your son did a good job and I had no problems with how he handled his position. You can be proud of Jordan."

"Thank you, Tarke, for the kind words. Now, knowing my position here, Grandfather and I asked Tarke to bring you into the Knowing. This will make my life a lot easier."

Tarke receives a message from a crew member rushing in the room. Tarke quickly stands. Jordan, come with me, and they rush out.

Jordan's grandfather is looking at Jordan's parents. "Don't worry; they will take care of whatever the problem is. So, what do you think now?"

Jordan's mother looks at Jordan's father. "This is quite a bit different than we thought Jordan's future would be," she says with a smile.

"Yes, it is. I'm very pleased with where he is, and with what I'm hearing," Jordan's father says, looking happy with the news about his son.

"Yes, you should be. Jordan in my thoughts is going to places that you and I could only dream of. I have to back up a little. Other than letting you know what he is doing, college is out for him. Jordan has no need to go that route."

While Grandfather and Jordan's parents are talking, Tarke and Jordan are looking at a couple of the monitor screens watching Rick as he is walking through the woods towards Jordan's camping site.

"What is he up to now? I don't see him carrying anything," Jordan says, as he is watching Rick.

Tarke, looking at the screens, "we will have to keep an eye on him to see what he is up to."

They both watch the screens, one is an expanded view, and the other is a close-up view. Rick gets close to the campsite and stops. They move the monitor view around and what do they see is an outdoor game camera cleverly attached to a tree.

"Turn the volume up; Tarke tells the screen operator." They can now hear Rick.

"I hope I have something." He opens up the camera and pushes a couple of buttons." Rick jumps back, "Look at this. I got them, the whole dang family and that Brayden kid also." He quickly unhooks the camera from the tree and looks around. "None of those jerks are here to stop me today."

He quickly rushes over to another tree to find his other game camera. After opening it and taking a look at any pictures, he turns to see if anyone is around. "Yes! I have the payday here. I have the entire alien family. Payday," he unstraps the camera from the tree and starts heading back to his car as fast as he can go.

Jordan, looking at Tarke, "you have more experience than me. What can we do?"

Tarke looking at Jordan, "I'm on it. Pete has Karen and they are on their way to intercept him."

Jordan looking at Tarke, "then what will she do?"

"No problem; we have disabled his car. He isn't going anywhere," answers Tarke. "Karen can take care of his pictures."

They look at the video screens as Rick is getting close to his car with both cameras in his hands.

Pete in the Explorer looks at Karen. "Let's teleport you down here."

"This will be good; I have the portable electronic disabler. I'll see you in a few." Karen teleports down slightly in a wooded area just off the road about one hundred yards in front of Rick's car.

Karen steps out to the side of the road to see Rick getting into his vehicle. She knows that his car isn't going to start and casually walks towards Rick in the car. Rick is now pounding on the steering wheel in frustration.

Karen walks up to the side of the car, looking at Rick. "Are you having problems?" she asks.

"Yeah, this darn piece will not start," he says in an angry voice.

Karen is looking in the car and can see the two game cameras in the seat next to Rick. Karen pulls out of her pocket what looks like a phone. "Do you want me to call for some help?"

Rick turns and looks at Karen, "hey, you can get the heck out of here! You are one of Jordan's alien friends." he says, after thinking that she might be, and he isn't going to take any chances.

"Hey, don't be so rude. I was just trying to help," she steps back and starts to walk away.

Rick gets out of his car turning to Karen, as she is walking away. "Keep going, Alien. Hey, tell your space cadets that I have what I need to uncover your activities." He reaches into his pocket and pulls out his phone. "What the heck! My phone is dead, also."

Karen keeps walking a short distance away, then steps back into the woods. "Pete, I'm coming up," she teleports into the Explorer. "I zapped his pictures and his phone just because he is such a great guy," she says with a smile.

Tarke and Jordan had been watching Karen and Rick.

"Rick isn't a very nice fella," says Tarke.

"You have that right. Wait until he finds that his hay-day pictures are gone."

Karen sends a message to Tarke. *Everything has been taken care of,* Tarke replies. *Thanks, when you get back come to the conference room.*

Jordan and Tarke look at each other with a smile. "Let's head back to the conference room."

They walk back in the room and take their seats.

Grandfather looks at them, "everything is taken care of?"

Jordan looks at Grandfather and his parents. "Remember that Rick guy? He had snuck into our campsite and placed two game cameras where we wouldn't normally see them." He looks at Tarke. "Tarke got a notice that Rick was walking to the campsite. We rushed out to see what he was up to. That is when we could see him getting his cameras that he had hidden in the trees."

Tarke looks at them, "when we first noticed Rick heading towards Jordan's campsite, I then sent Pete and Karen to take care of any potential problem."

Karen walks into the conference room.

"Hi, Karen, thanks for a good job," says Tarke.

Jordan is looking at Karen, "have a seat and please give us your report."

Karen looks at Jordan, "I have to start out with saying that this Rick guy sure isn't a nice fella."

"You have that right. I keep trying to be nice to him, but it just doesn't seem to have positive results," says Jordan.

"Yes, I agree. With that noted, we sent a signal down to Rick's car erasing its computer's memory. With this action, it disabled the engine from starting. Pete was able to let me teleport a short distance in front of him so I could walk by him."

Jordan's dad listing to Karen, "teleport?" he asks.

"Yes, John, we do have that capability."

"All of this is going to take a little while to soak in. Sorry for interrupting, please continue."

"No problem," she says; then turns back to Jordan. "I walked up to him as he was sitting in his car having a fit. It didn't take long for him to figure out who I was and he started in on me. At that time, I had the disabler ready and shot the cameras, erasing their memory. Rick started with his nasty behavior on me, so I adjusted the disabler to high power." Karen looks at Tarke, "I'm sorry, Tarke, but I felt that this had to be done. I hit the button on the disabler again and fried the cameras electronics. After thinking about it, I probably fried the electronics in everything that was in and around Rick's car."

"So, that is why when he tried to make a call, his phone didn't work," says Jordan.

"He was not a nice person when we first saw him at Jordan's campsite," Jordan's father says.

Tarke stands, "Gloria and John, it's time to get off of this subject. How about a tour of our ship?"

Jordan's father looks at Mother, "come on, let's take the tour with Tarke."

They get up and walk out of the conference room with Tarke.

"I'm going to see what Brayden is up to," says Jordan, as he stands, "How about you, Karen?"

"I have some things that I have to do. Maybe I'll catch up with you later."

Tarke and Jordan's parents walk off on their tour of the ship, as Jordan heads out to find Brayden. Jordan walks into the leisure room to see Brayden sitting with three of the crew members.

"Hi. Is Brayden telling you stories?" asks Jordan.

One crew member turns to Jordan, "he's a good storyteller." He looks back to Brayden with a smile, "he told us about when he dressed up as a green alien and surprised your mother."

"Oh, yes, that was a sight to behold," says Jordan.

The other crew member looks at Jordan. "He told us that he would wear it here someday."

"Brayden, you didn't."

"Yep, I did, it would be fun. I bet I would get a big laugh," answers Brayden.

There was a lot of laughter as Brayden went on telling his stories about his costume, and the many times at camp giving Jordan a hard time.

Jordan's parents received a good tour of the ship with Tarke.

It was a good time for everyone visiting the ship; then Jordan returned Brayden and his parents back home.

Learning time

Jordan returned his parents back home. The next day was time for the family to have a good talk about everything that has happened. Jordan is sitting in the living room with his mother and father.

"Well, you sprung a good one on us the other day," says Jordan's father.

Jordan looks at his father, "it was good, wasn't it?"

Mother adds her comment, "you have been full of surprises in the last week."

"Yes, Mom, after a few talks and working with them on the ship, there was a lot of planning to be able to get you to where you are now."

"I can believe that," Father agrees." Now I'm really interested in where you will go from here. I don't mean in space, but in charge of your own ship."

Jordan is looking at both of them. "I'm in suspense, also; I have a lot more to learn. The main thing now is that I can let you know when I'm going to be gone."

"Yes, that is good; but I still can worry about you," says Mother.

"I won't worry so much. You are in very trustworthy and capable hands," replies Jordan's father.

"Yes, they are; and, Mother, their main belief is no fighting."

"That's good to hear."

"I might as well start now. Tomorrow I will be going to the main ship and will stay there for a couple of days for some more training."

Mother, looking at Jordan, "you learn fast; you'll do well."

"Yes, Mother, I will learn fast." He looks at his father. "Did Tarke show you the medical room?" asks Jordan.

"Yes, he did, but he didn't go into depth about it."

"I'll tell you what I know about it. This is where a person called Harec works. I don't think that you have met Harec, he is a high-tech medical person. For learning large amounts of information, the medical room is where I go. Harec has a machine that will add information and knowledge to my brain. The amazing thing is that it happens in minutes."

"So, is that how they teach you?" Father asks.

"Mostly, yes. After a learning session, Tarke gives me helpful guidance."

"That's good to hear," says mother.

"As an example, in one learning session, I saw their world. It's like I have been there and spent a long time, maybe even lived there. I know the people, I know the buildings, everything. It's amazing! I have met the Elders on the main ship; they are the rulers of their world. And... when I met them, I knew them by name and had seen them before in my brain. Knowing that I had never really met them, I still knew who they were."

"Their technology has to be something else," Father says in amazement.

"Yes, it is, and I believe that is what I'm going to learn in the next day or two."

They talk about Jordan's experiences for another hour or so. Then they call it a night.

The next morning Jordan is up and getting ready to go to the ship. He cleans up and heads to the kitchen for his breakfast.

Mother is sitting at the table with a cup of coffee. "Good morning," she says with a smile.

"Good morning, has Dad left to go to work?"

"Yes, he left a half hour ago. He asked me to tell you, have a good time and learn a lot. He will talk to you in a couple of days."

"I'll give him a full report the next time I see him," Jordan says with a big smile.

Jordan finishes his breakfast and puts his dishes in the dishwasher, then gives his mother a hug. "I'm going to head out; I'll see you in a couple of days."

Jordan heads out the door and up to the campsite, where he will have his Explorer pick him up.

Upon arriving at the main ship, Jordan can see Tarke talking to a crew member by the monitor screens.

He walks over by Tarke. "Good morning," Jordan says.

Tarke looks around at Jordan. "Good morning, we are keeping an eye on Rick, he just came back to his home, by taxi."

"His car must be in the shop for repairs," says Jordan with a small grin on his face.

"Yes, Jordan. Karen did a job on him the other day."

Jordan, looking at Tarke, "so what are your thoughts on what she did?"

Tarke thinks for a minute, "well, it was a little harsh, I must say. But on the other hand, he was asking for it." he looks around, "there was no violence, so I'm good with what Karen did."

Rick lives by himself in a small apartment; he is sitting there on his second-hand couch thinking about what happened with his car and everything else the last time that he tried to get his proof of aliens.

"Dang it, I know that alien girl had something to do with destroying everything." He mutters out loud, "I spent over three hundred dollars for those two game cameras! And now they are junk!" he gets up to get the cameras, thinking that he is going to return them as faulty. "There is no reason normally that these things could fry themselves. That is what I'm going to do. The store can eat this junk, instead of me." He keeps talking to himself. "My phone, my watch, and my car! They are all fried! Those aliens don't want to see me again! This is going to cost me; I'm going to make sure it costs Jordan and his alien friends!"

Rick stomps around his apartment most of the day trying to come up with an alien proof idea to pay them back. In the meantime, his car will not be done at the repair shop for a week; they tell him. This is cooking up his anger.

Back at the ship Harec and Jordan are getting ready for another learning session.

Jordan is sitting in his familiar place in the medical room. Harec is dialing things in as he is getting ready to install some valuable information in Jordan's brain.

"Okay, Jordan, are you ready?" asks Harec.

"Yes, sir. I can't wait to go through this session," replies Jordan. He knows that this time is all about all of the technical abilities that he will have available.

"Relax, here you go." Harec turns on the transmitter.

Jordan sits back with a smile as things start flowing through his thoughts. Gadgets and unseen powers, with how to use, followed by why not to use everything. It is all flowing into his brain fast. With what is going into his brain, he doesn't have time to study it all; this will come together later.

Jordan is sitting there looking out into the room, as Harec is shaking his shoulder. "Come out of it, Jordan," he is saying.

Jordan looks over to Harec, "I was obviously thinking about everything that I just learned."

"It is a lot of information, it comes quickly and doesn't give you time for processing," says Harec. "It will settle in, in time, and then you will be able to use your new knowledge."

Harec removes the transmitter from around Jordan's head so Jordan can stand.

"Thanks, Harec. I do enjoy these learning sessions," he starts walking to the door, "I'll talk to you later, I'm sure."

Jordan walking out of the medical room can see Tarke coming his way. They meet down the hall.

"Jordan, I was coming to get you. I also want to talk to Harec. Let's meet in the conference room. I'm going to get Harec and we will meet you there."

"Okay, I'm going to stop and get a drink. Then I'll meet you there," replies Jordan.

Tarke heads off to get Harec, as Jordan walks into the leisure room and to the drink dispenser.

Jordan is coming out of the leisure room to see Tarke and Harec walking by at the same time. Together they walk to the conference room and take seats.

What's up, Jordan wonders. "What brings us here today?"

Tarke looks at Harec, "you gave Jordan the technology session today?"

"Yes, sir, I did," Harec replies.

"Good, I think that it is time and there is now knowledge that Jordan can use. With our problems with Rick, some of the powers may come in handy."

Harec looks at Jordan and then to Tarke, "so you want me to activate them?"

Tarke is looking at Harec, "yes, Harec, activate Jordan's medallion please." Then he turns to Jordan, "today you will have every power available to you that is available in your medallion."

"Is there anything else?" Harec asks.

"Yes, activate his ring to allow him to access every resource on the ship. This is my order; you can put this in your log. Thank you, Harec, you can go now."

Harec stands from his seat, "Congratulations, Jordan, you have made it to the top of authority." Harec walks out of the room.

Jordan is now thinking, *Wow, this has been easy!*

Tarke looks at Jordan, "easy you think," he says with a smile, "now is the hard part. This is knowing when and to what degree you will use your new position and powers that are available to you." Tarke stands from his seat, "I can see the day when I will make an announcement that you will be officially second in command of this ship. You are doing a wonderful job here and I have been listening to you and your thoughts all along so far."

"You have been listening to everything?" Jordan asks.

"Okay, we need to continue a bit more today." Tarke sits back down.

"Jordan, I take my job here very seriously. In order for me to make high priority decisions, I have to be clear with my decisions." He looks straight at Jordan. "You are on my high priority list. Yes, I have your medallion tuned into every thought that you make." Tarke looks up, "remember this morning when you were talking to your mother? You told her that you would give your father the full report the next time you see him," Tarke smiles.

Jordan smiles, "your listening to my thoughts for some time, and now giving me your trust and support, feels good."

"As you were taught today, you now have the ability to listen to anyone who is wearing a medallion. Use this ability wisely; this is a privilege that only a chosen few have."

Day with Brayden

It was a good time on the main ship. Working with Tarke was good after the learning session. Jordan has been given the ability to use all of the amazing technology aboard the ship, and with his ring, he has full access to everything. He knows that he has the powers and technology at his fingertips. It's just having the skills to know when and how to use these resources that is on his mind. He thinks that with Tarke's knowledge and help he will learn the skills to use the resources that are now available.

Jordan picks up his phone and calls Brayden. "Hi Brayden, I'm home. Come on over; I have a lot to tell you."

"Sure, I have been wondering about your last learning session. I'll be over in a few."

"Okay, I'll be out on the porch waiting for you." They both hang up their phones and Jordan walks out to the front porch and takes a seat.

About fifteen minutes later, here comes Brayden on his bike. He puts his bike by the garage and walks to the front porch then takes a seat next to Jordan.

"So what's up?" he asks.

Jordan smiles as he looks at Brayden. "My parents are in the Knowing, so we can talk without worrying about them hearing us. That feels so good."

"You have that right. My parents may never know about me being in the Knowing," says Brayden.

"Well, you never know. There might be a time?"

Brayden asks, "So, what's new?"

Jordan looks out at the road, "Oh not much, other than Tarke gave me full access to everything on the ship."

"Everything?" Brayden says with a surprised look.

"Yes, everything. My medallion now has full powers that only Tarke and I have access to use. He also gave my ring the power to access everything on the ship." Jordan says as he turns to Brayden.

"So that's what you wanted to tell me. We are going to have to celebrate."

"I'm going to order a pizza; are your parents' home?" Brayden asks.

"Just Mom; Dad's at work," Jordan answers.

"I don't care; I'm going to order two pizzas anyway. That way there will be some left over for your father."

Brayden takes his phone out of his pocket and dials the number for the pizza shop and places his order.

"Let's go in and tell your mother that we have pizzas coming."

"Okay, I guess we should let Mom know," and they both get up and head into the house.

"Hi, Mom." Brayden says, as he spots Jordan's mother when he walks into the house. "I just ordered two pizzas, so don't plan on making anything to eat this afternoon."

"You did; that was nice," says Mother.

"We are going to celebrate Jordan's promotion," says Brayden.

"Promotion? You didn't tell us that you received a promotion." Mother says as she looks at Jordan.

"I hadn't really had a chance. I was waiting for both you and Dad to be together before I told you the news."

They all go to the living room and take seats.

Mother looks at Jordan, "Okay, what kind of promotion did you get?"

Jordan looks at Mother, "it's a usage promotion right now."

"What is a usage promotion?" she asks with a questioning look.

"I'm still at the same rank, second in command trainee. Tarke gave me the power to access everything on the ship and gave me full power of my medallion."

"As second in command, you didn't have access to everything?" she asks.

"Yeah, I was wondering that also," says Brayden.

"Remember that I went to the ship this week for another learning session." Jordan looks at both Brayden and his mother. "This session was all about technology and how it can be used. I'm not really second in command. I'm now training to be second in command. This training session just brings me one step closer to that position."

"Now that had to be interesting," says Brayden.

"It was very interesting; now that I know what technical powers are available. Tarke gave me the ability to use them, but I will be hesitant to use them without Tarke's guidance."

"Yeah, you don't want to dissolve Rick," Brayden says smiling at Jordan.

Jordan smiles back, "well, there have been times."

Mother isn't into all the technical stuff, so she is now just sitting there listening to Jordan and Brayden.

"So tell me about the powers," Brayden says as he sits back in his chair.

"Well, there are too many things that they can do. It would take me two weeks to brush through everything. You have seen teleporting. I've told you about my learning sessions." Jordan sits back for a moment thinking about everything that he has learned, and then looks at Brayden. "They were able to disable Rick's car from the Explorer. Karen was able to destroy Rick's pictures without touching his cameras."

Brayden looks at Jordan with a grin, "and I heard that she zapped his phone, also."

Jordan chuckles, "she turned the power up in the electronics disabler a little bit too high and fried everything electronic in and around Rick's car."

Brayden gives Jordan a questioning look and asks. "his car, too?"

"Yes, sir, everything, even his car," Jordan replies.

Brayden, looking at Jordan, "he can't be a happy guy right now."

The doorbell rings and Brayden jumps up. "It's the pizza, I bet." He rushes to the door and opens it.

There stands a pizza delivery man with two pizza boxes. "Hi, sir, here are your two large deluxe pizzas."

Brayden takes the pizzas and pays the delivery man. He puts them on the kitchen table and heads back to the living room. "That was the pizza delivery; I put them on the kitchen table."

"Thank you, Brayden, I'll go ahead and take care of them," says Mother.

"Keep one out; I'm hungry. How about you, Jordan?"

"Sounds good to me," and they both follow Mother into the kitchen.

It was a good meal with a nice discussion about Jordan's promotion. They left more than enough pizza for Jordan's father when he gets home.

Revenge

Rick receives a call from the auto repair shop.

"Hi, Rick, I don't have good news for you. We made a thorough check of your vehicle and the cost of repair is more than the value of it."

Rick stomps his feet on the floor. "What?"

"Yes, everything electrical is melted. What did you do, or what happened?" the mechanic asks.

Rick stands there for a moment thinking, *how do I explain this?* "An alien did it," he tells the mechanic.

"Okay, that's good enough of an excuse for me," the mechanic thinking he isn't going to get anything out of Rick. "We are going to move your vehicle to the back lot."

"Do that then; I'll contact another repair shop to fix it. Apparently, you guys can't," Rick says with an angry voice.

The shop mechanic replies, "Okay, do what you want. I'll give you two days to remove the vehicle before I start charging storage."

Rick doesn't say anything and hangs up the phone. He walks over to his couch and plops down in anger talking to himself. "It cost me a bundle for my new phone," he says loudly. "Now my car is fried!" he gets up and stomps around the apartment, slamming doors. "I can't afford a new car." He kicks his table, "I'm going to go and return those two faulty pieces of junk cameras."

Rick picks up the cameras off the table; he had put them back into their original boxes. Throwing them into a bag, he heads out the door. He takes a few steps out of the apartment and realizes that he doesn't have a car. He swings around and heads back into the apartment, slamming the door behind him.

Jordan has an idea and calls Brayden.

"Hi, Brayden. Hey, I have been thinking."

Brayden quickly replies, "you have enough room in your brain to think?" he says with a chuckle.

"Yes, I do... I don't have to pay for college."

"You mean that we can take a ride to the sporting goods store?" he asks, figuring out what Jordan is thinking.

"Yes, let's go. I'll call the trolley and have them stop and pick you up."

Brayden asks, "when?"

"I'll call them now; how is that?"

Brayden replies, "I'll be out front waiting. One thing though I don't have any money. It's all in the credit union."

"Don't worry about it; I'll cover it. You can pay me back when you get the money."

They hang up their phones and Jordan calls for the trolley. An hour later they are on their way to the sporting goods store.

They have the trolley driver that has taken them to the beach many times, and they have had many discussions with him. He looks back at them through his rearview mirror. "So, you're not going to the beach today?"

Brayden replies, "As you know, we are going to the sporting goods store. We are going to purchase our own kiteboarding equipment today," he says with a big smile.

"That sounds great. I'll get you there in just a few minutes. No more renting?"

"Yes, the only thing is that we will miss renting from Tom. He is a good guy," says Jordan.

"I bet you will still see him from time to time," the driver replies. "Okay, here is your stop."

Brayden stands from his seat. "We'll give you a call later." And Jordan and Brayden get off the trolley and head for the sporting goods store.

Brayden looks at Jordan as they approach the store door. "This is going to be fun," the door opens and they walk in.

Jordan grabs Brayden by the arm, pulling him to the side quickly. They go over a couple of aisles. "I see Rick's over at the service counter."

Brayden looks back, "did he see us?"

"I don't know," Jordan says as he tries to move out of Rick's sight. "I think that he is trying to return those two game cameras, that Karen fried," he says with a grin. "Let's go find the kiteboarding equipment. Hopefully, he won't see us back there."

"Okay, let's go. I don't want to have anything to do with him," says Brayden as he quickly heads back to the equipment.

They go to the back of the store and start looking around.

"I have only looked at this stuff online," says Brayden, as he is checking everything out.

A sales person walks up to them, "Hi, can I help you with anything?"

Brayden answers, "yes, we are interested in buying some kiteboarding equipment," as he is looking at everything.

"Yes, we need everything. We have taken lessons and have been renting all summer so far," Jordan tells him.

"So, I bet you have been renting from Tom," he says.

Jordan answers, "yes, we have. He also taught us how to kiteboard."

The clerk looks at them, "Tom's a good guy and a good instructor, He sends a lot of his students here." he walks over by some display kites. "I would recommend the freeride style; we have these on sale this month." He points to one on display. "Freerides are adjustable to several conditions and are a great all-around kite."

Jordan and Brayden look them over; there are several different color styles.

Brayden looks at the clerk, "no alien green?" he asks.

"Sorry, we just have blue, red and green styles. Our sale includes everything, including the board, kite, bag, and pump." He looks at Jordan, "seventeen ninety-five. It's normally a twenty-two hundred dollar, outfit."

Jordan and Brayden are looking at their choices and Jordan notices Rick coming their way. Jordan thinks for a minute, remembering his lesson and the powers that he has in his medallion. Jordan tells Brayden, "stand back."

Rick walks up to them with an angry look. "So here are the alien lovers! You guys cost me a lot of money." He walks up to Jordan and stands closely face to face with him. "You're going to pay."

The store clerk stands back and calls for security.

Jordan looks straight at Rick, as he is thinking, *I'll take care of you.* He thinks a message into his medallion, *wipe out Rick's total memory for a half hour.*

Jordan looks at the clerk, "don't worry about him, he has a few screws loose. We don't need security." Jordan looks at Brayden, "why don't you walk him over by the camping stuff and set him in one of those folding chairs."

Brayden looks at Jordan and then at Rick with a puzzled look. "Okay," then he grabs Rick by the arm as Rick is just standing there with a blank look, looking out into the store. "Come on, Rick," he walks him over and sets him down in one of the display camping chairs.

Jordan stands there with a huge smile as Brayden walks back. Jordan sends Brayden a message; *I'll tell you how later.*

The store clerk looks at Jordan, "are you sure that he is going to be okay? He didn't act normal when he walked up to you."

As Brayden walks back by them he answers with a smile, "he isn't normal."

Jordan replies, "we have had problems with him thinking that we are aliens." He looks over at Rick just sitting there. "Rick will be okay in a little while when he comes out of his spell. Just let him figure out where he is; then he will get up and go home."

"That's crazy; I have never seen anything like that," says the clerk as he looks at Rick. "So, how about our sale? It's a good deal, and you only have a few days left to decide."

Jordan looks at Brayden, "I have the money; what do you think?"

"I like the red one. It looks like the same one that Tom has rented to us," answers Brayden.

Jordan looks at the display sample, then back to Brayden and the store clerk. "Okay, we will take the red one."

The clerk replies, "good. You will like it. Give me a couple minutes to go to the back room and get your equipment." Then he walks off.

Brayden looks at Jordan, "what the heck did you do to Rick? He is still sitting there like a rag doll."

Jordan looks at Rick, then back to Brayden. "I totally erased his memory for a half hour," he says with a smile.

"I can't help myself," then Brayden walks off towards Rick.

Jordan is watching Brayden as he heads over by the beach items near where Rick is sitting. He grabs a big pink flowered beach hat; then walks over, puts it on Rick's head and then looks back at Jordan with a big smile.

Jordan could only watch Brayden, knowing his humor, as Brayden walks back.

The store clerk comes back with a kite bag and puts it on the counter. "I went through everything for you and added the pump. It's all here." He opens up the bag showing them everything, "I unboxed everything and put it all into the bag for you, thinking that it would be easier for you to carry home."

Jordan and Brayden check everything out, "thanks it looks good," says Jordan as he looks at Brayden for his approval.

"Good, now I can't wait to try it out."

They pay for their new kiteboarding equipment and head for the door. They walk by Rick sitting there wearing the big pink hat. Brayden stops looking at him, laughing, "don't mess with us, icky Rickie," and they leave him sitting there in his suspended state.

They walk out of the store and call the trolley, as they both receive a message from Tarke. *Okay, we have been here listening to you two. I wish that I could have seen it.*

Brayden messages back, *you will, I'll go back in, and take a picture for you.* Brayden rushes back in to get the picture.

The trolley pulls up, and they get in with their new kiteboarding equipment with Brayden smiling, as he is looking at the picture on his phone.

Aftermath

Jordan and Brayden are on their way home with big grins on their faces and not saying much.

The driver looks back at them during a stop. "You two look like a cat that just caught a mouse."

Brayden answers, as he glances at Jordan, "yes, we did."

"I see that you must have purchased your kiteboard stuff."

Jordan answers, "yes, they had them on sale." He looks at Brayden thinking him a message; *we sure did get the mouse; he has to be just coming out of his thoughtless state.*

Brayden looks at Jordan smiling, as he nods his head.

Back at the store:

Rick is still sitting there, as he starts looking around with a dazed look on his face.

The sales clerk is near and has been watching him. He walks over to Rick, "can I help you?" he asks.

Rick looks up at him, still dazed and not knowing where he is. "ah... what?" he says, as he looks up at the sales clerk.

The clerk is standing there trying his very best not to crack a smile, as he is looking at Rick wearing the big pink hat; knowing that the two guys that just purchased the kiteboarding equipment put the hat on him. "There's a mirror over there," he points to a mirror on a stand, "you can use it to see if that hat you have on is what you want."

Rick reaches up to find a hat on his head. He takes it off to look at it." He is now coming out of it and takes the hat, throws it on the floor and quickly stands.

The store clerk steps back, watching Rick, not knowing what he might do.

Rick looks around, "I'm out of this stupid place." He stumbles the first couple steps, then picks up his pace, and away he goes.

The store clerk watching him leave, breaks out into laughter.

Brayden stays on the trolley to Jordan's home and gets off with him.

They take the kiteboarding equipment in the house to show Jordan's mother. As they enter, Jordan finds a note. "Jordan I went shopping with my friends."

Jordan looks at Brayden, "Mom's shopping."

Brayden, looking out the window, "let's put the kite stuff in your room and then take a walk. I have a few things that I want to ask you."

They put the equipment into Jordan's closet and head out to the back yard. Then they take a seat at the picnic table. "Now, what exactly did you do to that Rick guy?" asks Brayden.

"Thank goodness for the last learning session. It taught me how to use all the features of my medallion."

Brayden looking at Jordan, "and wiping out someone's memory is one of them?"

Jordan answers, "yes, it is. It is an option not intended to be used in the manner that I used it. It would normally be used for... I'll give you an example. If someone saw the Explorer, I could erase their memory and they would never remember seeing it."

Brayden smiles, "so he doesn't have any idea that he had ever seen us in the sporting store." Now that's good thinking. "To change the subject just a little, I have been thinking, our medallions... when we are at the beach, it's a bit awkward to wear it when we are swimming or kiteboarding."

"We don't have to wear them all the time, and we don't," Jordan replies.

Brayden looks at Jordan, "that's the problem. When we put them in our bags, what's to say that they won't come up missing some day?"

"I suppose that could happen. They can be traced very quickly," Jordan answers.

"I'm sure that they can, but what kind of problem would that create? My idea is to make a medallion style waterproof watch. What do you think about that?"

"Now, that's a very good idea. Tarke, did you hear that?" Jordan says.

Brayden turns to Jordan with a questioning look, "did you just message Tarke with my idea?"

"No, I didn't have to. I'm sure that Tarke is listening to us right now." Both Jordan and Brayden receive a reply, *yes, Brayden I did hear your idea and now wonder why we didn't think of it.* Jordan replies, *we told you that he is smart.* Tarke answers, *I agree, thanks, Brayden, for a good idea. I will send the idea to our technicians for their approval and hopeful development. By the way, Jordan, I liked your quick thinking when Rick confronted you, and it was a creative use of the erase memory function. Good job.* Jordan replies, *thanks, Tarke, I had to think quickly. He was in my face, with me not knowing what he was going to do.*

Rick walks out of the store and stands there trying to figure out what happened. He walks over to a bench, takes a seat and looks out into the parking lot. He reaches into his pocket and finds a lot of money along with his phone. Looking at all the money he is wondering, what is this? He grins and puts it back in his pocket thinking, *I don't remember where I got this, but I'll keep it.* He takes his phone and calls for a taxi to take him home.

All the way home he kept trying to figure out why he was at the store and it was really bugging him.

The taxi drops him off and leaves as Rick heads into his apartment. Upon entering all he can see is a mess with stuff strewn all over the place. He sits down looking around the room just wondering what the heck happened today.

A visit

The next day Brayden comes over to Jordan's house, unannounced, on his bike. He pushes the doorbell once and opens the door to see Jordan's mother in the kitchen.

"Hi, Mom."

Jordan's mother looks over and replies, "He's in his room," she answers knowing why he is here.

"Thanks." Brayden heads to find Jordan.

He walks into Jordan's room, to find him half asleep on his bed.

"Wake up, sleepy head," he says, as he sits down on the edge of the bed.

Jordan sits up, "I wasn't sleeping."

"Yeah, the heck you weren't. I could hear you snoring all the way down the hall," he says with a grin. Brayden reaches into his pocket and pulls out some money. "Here is my half for the kiteboard; I stopped at the credit union on my way here." He hands Jordan the money. "Let's go to Grandpa's. I can't wait to tell him what you did to Rick." Brayden stands, "I have been chuckling about it all night long. I couldn't sleep and kept looking at the picture which I took of him."

Jordan gets up from the bed. "Yes, I thought about it also; it was funny. Not only the hat, but how I was able to stop him in his tracks." He starts for the door, "let's go before I go back to sleep. Are you coming?" he turns with a smile.

It didn't take them long riding their bikes to Grandpa's house, to see grandmother outside pulling weeds out from around her flowers.

"Hi, Grandma," says Jordan as he parks his bike.

"Hi, boys. Grandfather is down in his room," she says as she pulls up another weed.

"Hi, Grandmother," says Brayden as they go in the house.

Down to the lower level they go and with a knock on the door, they go in. There sits Grandpa at his workbench with a soldering iron in his hand.

He turns, "Hi, boys; what's up today?"

Jordan answers, "We went out and purchased new kiteboarding equipment yesterday," he says with a smile.

Brayden can't wait to tell Grandpa about Rick. "Guess who we saw at the sporting goods store?" he says, looking at Grandpa.

Grandfather turns to Brayden, "who did you see?"

"Rick!" he says.

Grandfather looks over at Jordan. "That couldn't have been fun."

"Brayden, will you go shut the door, please?" Brayden quickly goes over and shuts the man's room door.

"Thanks. I have to say, it was fun." Jordan turns to Brayden, "go ahead and tell him about what happened. I know that you are busting at the seams."

Brayden, looking at Grandpa with a smile, "Jordan froze him right in his tracks!" he looks at Jordan. "Rick was right up in Jordan's face and zap! He could only stand there with a stupid look on his face.

Jordan smiles with Brayden's description of what happened. "My last learning session along with Tarke giving me full powers with my medallion. I just shut down Rick's brain for thirty minutes."

"That was good thinking," Grandpa replies.

Brayden, still itching to continue, "Jordan asked me to take icky Ricky over to the camping display in the store. So, I did, and put him down on a camp chair."

Jordan smiles, "tell him what you did next."

Brayden looks at Grandpa and walks over to the table like he is getting something. "I saw a hat display," Brayden reaches up like he is grabbing something. "There was a big pink floppy woman's flowered hat on the rack. I took it and put it on Rick."

Jordan and Brayden start to laugh remembering Rick sitting there with the big pink hat.

Brayden takes his phone out of his pocket and looks for his picture of Rick. "Here is the picture of Rick," as he shows it to Grandpa.

Grandpa chuckles remembering Rick. " Now that's a nice picture." He looks at Jordan, "you had to make a quick decision."

Jordan thinking back, "Yes, I didn't know what he was going to do. So, to erase his memory was my best option. Like Brayden says," Jordan smiles, "I zapped him."

Brayden replies, "He sure did! I just stood there alongside of the sales person in the store and watched icky Ricky freeze." Brayden freezes in his place, standing like a statue.

"I figured that Jordan did something but didn't know what."

Grandpa, smiling as he watches Brayden act out his descriptions, "what did the salesman say?"

"He didn't know what happened and had no idea of Jordan's powers," Brayden replies with a smile.

"I just told the salesman that it often happens with Rick and just let him sit there for a while. He will come around in a while and just get up and leave."

Grandpa looks at Brayden, to see if there is going to be another show. "I hope for the store's sake, that is what he did."

Jordan, grinning, "When his brain came back alive, it probably took Rick a while to figure out where he was. I'm sure he stumbled out wondering what happened."

Brayden, looking at Jordan, "I need to show Tarke my picture," he says as he pulls out his phone and looks at Rick's picture.

Jordan, smiling, knowing that Tarke probably has been listening to Brayden. "Yes, Brayden, I should go to the ship and report what happened to Tarke."

"That would be a good idea, Jordan. You two should go and visit your grandmother," Grandpa tells them.

Brayden replies, "That's a good idea, let's go and help Grandma pull weeds."

Jordan agrees and with a see-you-later, they head out front to find Grandmother.

Rick's company

After sitting for a while, Rick's memory slowly comes back. He is sitting there looking around his apartment thinking. *That money is from returning those game cameras that those Aliens destroyed.* He smiles, *that stupid guy in the store gave me my money back.* Rick sits there thinking about the day. *I remember seeing that Jordan alien lover.* He thinks harder; *I did go back to confront him.* He can't remember any more. Rick sits there looking around trying to figure out what else happened? *That Jordan, ... did he do something to me? I didn't see any of his alien friends around that I can remember.*

Rick sat there trying his best to figure out what happened. How come he can't remember what seems like a good amount of time?

Jordan and Brayden return back to Jordan's home after helping Grandmother pull the weeds out from around her flowers.

Jordan looks over at Brayden, "let's go up to the campsite and I'll call my Explorer so we can give Tarke my report."

"Sounds good; let's go," replies Brayden.

Jordan quickly heads into the house and tells his mother where he is going.

Brayden walks to the backyard and sits down at the picnic table thinking. *It's just going to be Jordan and me in the Explorer. This is too cool.*

Jordan walks up to Brayden who is in deep thought and didn't notice him. "Quit daydreaming; let's go."

Brayden looks up, "I was just thinking that it's just going to be you and me flying the Explorer."

"I hadn't thought of it that way. I have flown it by myself; now that was an experience." Jordan says with a smile, as they head up to the campsite.

"Wow, that had to be strange," says Brayden, agreeing. "For someone who has never driven a car and now you are flying a UFO." He says with a smile as they are walking.

"Yes, our lives have changed quite a bit this summer. I guess I'll have to learn how to drive a car someday." Jordan grins.

They arrive at the campsite. Jordan had already summoned the Explorer and it was there waiting. All Jordan had to do is command it to become visible. With his command, they enter and take their seats.

Brayden can't help himself as he is looking out as they rise up over the trees. "This is just too cool," turning to Jordan. "You can just fly this wherever you want, can't you?"

Jordan answers, "well, yes and no. Yes, I can, it's my Explorer. But no, I shouldn't without letting Tarke or someone on the main ship know where I'm going if it's out of the normal."

It didn't take long as Jordan slowly sets the Explorer down into the water and heads for the ship.

They dock with the ship and head into the main corridor to see Tarke talking with one of the crew members.

Tarke turns to see them walking his way. "Hi, Jordan and Brayden. Let's go to the conference room." They head that way. "I have been listening to your conversations; I can't wait to hear them first hand."

Rick hears someone knocking at the door. He walks over and opens the door to see a well-dressed man with a briefcase standing there. "Can I help you?" he asks.

"I'm from the UFO investigation organization," he starts saying.

Rick quickly speaks up, "I have been looking forward to reporting a sighting. Come on in." Rick steps aside to allow him in.

The man walks into Rick's apartment. Rick had cleaned it up and had it looking nice, wanting to impress his expected visitor. "My name is Bill and you must be Rick. It's nice to meet you, Rick, I have read the report that you submitted," he says, as he looks around Rick's apartment. "How about we take a seat at your table. I have a few questions."

Rick looks over at his kitchen table, "sure that is fine."

Both of them take their seats. Bill opens up his briefcase and takes out a recorder and a few papers. "I would like to record our conversation if that is all right with you."

Rick answers, "that is okay with me; record away."

Bill brushes through his notes and with a pencil in hand he turns on the recorder. Looking at Rick, "Okay tell me what you saw."

Rick looks at Bill, "I'm a photographer and a couple weeks ago, I was walking through the lake front dunes snapping nature photos. As I was looking for shots, I spotted a friend of mine setting up a tent." Rick looks up, then down at the recorder. "I thought that I would sit down and wait until it was up. Then I would jump up and surprise him." He looks straight at Bill, "all of a sudden a UFO appeared on the ground by the tent stuff. Then an Alien came out of it. I grabbed my camera and started taking pictures."

Bill sits up straight looking at Rick, "I have to see your photos," he says thinking that they now have something.

Rick slams his hands on the table, startling Bill. "I don't have them! Those aliens somehow deleted them."

Bill can see that Rick is upset, "calm down Rick. Tell me more about when you were taking the pictures."

"I took a bunch of photo; then put my camera down. Then I had to see the UFO and the Alien, so I walked over to them," he explains.

"What did the UFO look like when you got close?" Bill asks with anticipation of maybe learning something new.

"When the alien came out of the UFO, it disappeared." Rick looks at Bill with a questioning look on his face.

"So, you couldn't have taken many pictures of the UFO?" asks Bill.

Rick gives Bill an angry look, "no, not a lot but I had pictures! And I also had the Alien coming out of it."

Bill looking at Rick, "you had to be brave to walk up to them."

"Yeah, they don't scare me. I talked to my friend and the alien for a couple minutes; then thought it would be best if I left so, I did. As I left, I casually picked up my camera that was behind a tree and walked off."

Bill writes down a couple notes, "So how many people and or aliens did you see?"

"Just my friend, Jordan, and the one Alien," Rick tells Bill, not telling the truth.

Bill looks up from his notes, "so when did you find out that you didn't have any pictures?" he asks.

Rick's truth-less story continues, "when I got home; I thought, *wow, I have pictures.* I sat down and turned on my camera." He looks at Bill, "there was nothing! Not one picture and I had taken at least 100 photos that day."

"Are you sure that your camera was working?"

Rick stands and gets his camera from by his couch. He walks back to the table and takes a quick picture of Bill. Rick walks around the table by Bill and shows him the picture that he just took. "There you go, Mr. Bill; it works."

"Okay, Rick, I believe you." Bill feeling the tension, wanting to change the subject, "I would like to see the area where you saw the UFO. Do you have time today to show me?"

"Yes, I do, but I don't have a car anymore." Rick turns at Bill with an angry look. "The aliens fried it!"

126

Bill closes his briefcase, thinking Rick supposedly didn't have a pleasant encounter with the aliens. "You haven't told me about that."

Rick continues with his angry look on his face, "I thought that I would hide a game camera by where I saw the Alien and UFO. I was hoping that he would come back in his UFO." Rick looks down, then up at Bill, "a couple days later I went back to check the camera. Bingo, I had the UFO and the whole darn family."

Bill looking at Rick, "family?"

"That's what I said. Jordan, his parents and the Alien."

"How about the UFO?" Bill asks.

Rick's gives Bill an angry glaring look. "Yes, I had the dang UFO, also."

Bill asks, "had?"

"Had; I don't stutter. I had the pictures! I took my camera and quickly went back to my car; just to find out that it would not start." Rick holds his arms out, "then an alien walked up and took something out of his pocket." He motions like he is pulling something out of his pocket. "He had something that fried everything that I had... everything electronic, my car, phone, camera and even my watch."

"So, I take it that the memory card in the camera was also ruined?" Bill asks.

"Everything, my car is now junk, the camera junk," replies Rick.

Bill, looking at Rick, "we can use my car. Let's take a ride and you can show me where you spotted the UFO."

Wanting to get the information that he needs for his investigation, Rick seems a bit too agitated today for Bill's liking.

They get into Bill's car and Rick directs him to where Jordan lives. Rick has Bill stop just before Jordan's driveway. "Okay, this is Jordan's home and behind the house up the hill is the spot."

Bill puts his car in park, "explain the spot to me, please."

Rick points to the hill, "up at the top of that hill, there is a campsite where Jordan sets up his tent. It's a large enough area where the UFO can land there."

Bill, looking at the hill, "I take it that the UFO isn't that big then."

"It's not that big; 3 or 4 aliens maybe," Rick says, as he is looking at Jordan's house.

Bill looks at Rick, "I didn't ask, what did the Alien look like?"

Rick looks at Bill with a grin, "you."

"Me," Bill asks with a puzzled look.

"Yep, like you and me. You could walk right by one and never know it," Rick says with a serious look. "It's time that you take me home."

"You don't want to stop in and have a talk with your friend? We might be able to get to the bottom of this."

"Nope, take me home," Rick says with an instant tone in his voice.

"Okay," Bill says, as he turns his car around.

Beach day

Jordan's mother is in the kitchen getting another cup of coffee and hears a knock at the door. She turns to see Brayden coming in. "Good morning," she says, as she finishes filling her cup.

"Hi, Mom," he says, as he puts his sports bag down and closes the door.

She looks up, "Jordan is in his room."

"Thanks," Brayden says, as he heads to Jordan's room.

He enters Jordan's room to see that he has the kiteboarding equipment out on his bed. Jordan is standing there checking everything out.

Brayden walks into Jordan's room, "is it all there?" he says, smiling.

Jordan looks over to Brayden, "yep, I think everything is here," smiling back. "I was going to give you a call, but I think you had the same idea."

Brayden looking at Jordan's bed with all the kiteboarding equipment laying on it. "You bet, that is why I'm here. My alien suit and everything is in my bag by the door." He looks over to Jordan, "where is your stuff?" he says with a smile.

"It's in my closet," Jordan walks over to get his stuff.

Brayden starts putting the kiteboarding equipment back into its bag; as Jordan checks to see if everything that he needs for the beach is in his sports bag.

Jordan closes his bag and looks at Brayden, "I have everything that I need; let's go."

Brayden picks up the kiteboarding equipment bag. "Let's go; you can carry my bag."

. "That's a deal," says Jordan, as they head out to tell Jordan's mother where they are going.

Mother is sitting in the living room with her cup of coffee and looking at one of Jordan's books.

Brayden looks at Jordan, then at Jordan's mother. "Found some good reading?" he says with a smile.

Mother looks up at Brayden, "yes, I do find Jordan's books a bit more interesting now," she says with a grin. "Looks like you two are going to the beach."

Jordan replies, "We are going to give our new kiteboard a try today."

"Be safe and have fun," she says, as she turns a page in the book.

Jordan picks up Brayden's sports bag and they head outside. Jordan stops and looks at Brayden, half laughing. "We didn't call for the trolley."

Brayden sets the kiteboarding equipment down and turns to Jordan. "I guess we should; it's a long walk to the beach."

"Let's go to the front porch and give the trolley a call," Jordan replies with a big smile.

Brayden picks up the equipment and they walk around to the front porch. They set things down as they take their seats. Jordan opens his bag and takes out his phone to give the trolley company a call. After talking to them, he turns to Brayden, "they told me that it will be a little over a half hour before they can pick us up."

Brayden answers, "Okay, there isn't much we can do about that. Let's count junkers as they go by."

They sit there watching the cars go by; then one pulls into the driveway.

Brayden looks at Jordan, "who is that?" he asks.

"I don't know; I don't recognize the car," Jordan says as the car stops. A tall, slender, well-dressed man steps out of the car with a briefcase in hand. He looks over and can see Jordan and Brayden sitting on the porch. He walks over to them with a happy look on his face.

"Hello, I'm Bill. It sure is a nice day today isn't it," he says.

Jordan stands, "Hi, Bill, what can I do for you?" he says, as he reaches out to shake his hand. "My name is Jordan and this is Brayden."

Bill shakes Jordan's hand. "Hi, Jordan. Hi, Brayden. It's nice to meet you. I'm from the UFO investigators' organization, and I'm traveling around the area seeking information on possible sightings."

Jordan looks at Brayden then back to Bill. "Has anyone seen one?" thinking a message to Brayden. *Here we go. Rick is behind this, I bet.*

Brayden grins as he looks at Bill, "I counted three so far today," he points out at the road. "There goes another one. Now that's an unidentified object for sure. That's number four."

Bill, watching the car go down the road, "Now that was unidentifiable."

Brayden quickly comes back with a question, "what brings you here, has anyone reported seeing one?"

Bill, still standing there with his briefcase in hand. "I'm just out searching for sightings. I will tell you this; anyone who reports any information is never disclosed to the public without their full approval."

Brayden replies, "So you won't tell us if someone has."

Jordan is just sitting there letting Brayden have at Bill with his humor and questions.

"I have had one report of a sighting so far in my investigations; that is as far as I will go." Bill remembers that Rick had mentioned Jordan. He turns to Jordan. "So, Jordan, you haven't said anything. Have you seen anything? By that, you know what I mean, any UFOs."

Jordan looks at Bill, "no I haven't seen an unidentified flying object." He tells Bill simply because they are identified flying objects to him now. This way he doesn't have to lie.

Brayden stands, "here comes our ride."

Jordan looks out at the road to see the trolley pull into the driveway. "It was nice to meet you, Bill. This is our ride to the beach; we have to go."

Bill, seeing the trolley stop in the driveway, turns to Jordan and Brayden. "Have a good time; maybe I'll see you again."

Jordan grabs the two sports bags and Brayden picks up the kiteboarding equipment. They walk to the trolley, get in and off they go as Bill stands there on the porch.

Jordan and Brayden go to the back of the trolley where they can put their bags down and they can talk.

The trolley driver looking back at them, "that's not your usual seat."

Jordan replies, "the kiteboarding equipment bag is longer than the seats, so we put it in the back seat."

Brayden thinks a message to Jordan; that was *good quick thinking.* Jordan gives Brayden a wink.

"Thanks, good thinking. I have a couple more stops on the way to the beach. I remember that it's your new kiteboard, isn't it?" he turns around and backs the trolley out of the driveway.

"Yes, it is. This will be our first time out with it," Jordan replies.

Brayden turns to Jordan changing the subject talking in a quiet voice. "I liked how you told that Bill guy that you have never seen an unidentified flying object. I got what you were thinking right away; they are identified to you and me." Brayden smiles and looks forward in the trolley.

"Yep, and two guesses who put him up to paying us a visit." Jordan looks at Brayden. "We are done with him today; now it's time to think kiteboarding."

Brayden, still looking forward, "I know, but his investigations aren't over I bet. He will be back and, like Rick, Bill is going to be someone else to deal with. Now with that said, I'll switch my thinking to kiteboarding."

They sat in the back of the trolley quietly for the rest of the ride.

The trolley stops, "here you go, guys. Have fun with your new kiteboard," says the trolley driver as he opens the door for them. They step out of the trolley and who do they see standing there; it's Karen. "Hi, guys. Tarke told me that you were going to go to the beach and he gave me time off to join you."

Jordan, looking at Karen with a big smile, "that was nice of him." Jordan has always liked Karen and is always happy to see her.

"Come on; we are going to try our new kiteboard," Brayden says as he heads over to the beach kiteboarding area. He looks around, "I don't see Tom here today."

Jordan and Karen following Brayden, "he could pop up anytime," Jordan replies.

Brayden walks over to a place on the beach where Tom has used to set up his kites. He turns to Jordan, "Tom isn't using this area today, what do you think about setting up here?"

Karen looks around, "Tom isn't here; why not. I can't wait to see you two aliens with your new kite," she says with a smile.

"Looks good to me," Jordan agrees and sets down their sports bags. "I can't wait; let's get this kite setup."

Brayden opens up the equipment bag and both of them start taking everything out.

"Is there anything that I can help you with?" Karen asks, as she stands there watching them.

Brayden looks up at Karen, "thanks for asking. It's our first time unpacking everything; maybe next time."

As Jordan is getting the kite in position, he stops and looks over at Karen with a grin, "Brayden and I will have to give you kiteboarding lessons."

"No, no, I'll be happy watching you two. That will be fun enough for me."

Jordan and Brayden work carefully setting the kite up, as Karen takes the kiteboard out of the equipment bag for them.

Brayden looks at Jordan, "it was your idea to finally get the kiteboard and you that initially paid for it. So, you get to be the first to use it."

"Thanks, Brayden. I'll be happy to take the maiden ride." He looks at Karen with a smile, "it's time to be an Alien," he grabs his sports bag and heads to the pavilion changing room.

It didn't take long for Jordan to get into his wetsuit. Out he comes carrying his sports bag, wearing his green wetsuit, with a big smile on his face.

Jordan puts the harness on and with Brayden's help the kite is up in the air. Brayden grabs the board and down to the water they go.

Jordan slips his feet into their place on the board. Then he lowers the kite down in the air to catch more air and off he goes.

Brayden and Karen stand there watching Jordan skip across the water with ease.

Karen, watching Jordan, "he is getting good at kiteboarding."

"Look at that Alien go," Brayden grins as he looks over at Karen. "We have had practice renting from Tom this summer."

They walk back to their stuff and take out their towels and sit down to watch Jordan.

Brayden sits there for a couple minutes then gets up. "I better get my alien wetsuit on before Jordan runs out of gas," he says as he picks up his sports bag.

"Good idea; I'll hold down the fort," Karen says, as she watches Jordan kiteboarding out on the lake.

A few minutes later, Brayden comes walking up and stands by Karen. He puts his hand behind his head standing in a modeling pose in his green wetsuit. "How is this for an Alien? I bet you have never seen one like this," he says smiling at Karen.

Karen looks Brayden over slowly, "nope, I have never seen an Alien like you before today," she says with a questioning look.

Brayden looks out on the lake for Jordan, "boy, he is way out there."

Karen replies, "yes, he has been going back and forth out there. It looks like he is working his way in towards shore now."

"I think that I'll walk to the shoreline just in case he decides to take a break."

"Okay, I'll just sit here and watch," Karen replies.

Brayden walks to the shoreline and gets there as Jordan comes to a stop close to him. "Wow, our new kiteboard is the best," he says, as he helps Brayden get ready for his first try.

With Jordan's help, Brayden is off flying across the water yelling as he goes. Jordan, smiling, turns and heads up towards Karen. As he gets close, he happens to see a man in the parking lot with a pair of binoculars looking his way. Jordan casually turns to Karen and sits down.

"Don't look back; there is a man watching us in the parking lot. It looks like Bill, a UFO investigator. He was at my house just before we came here."

Karen looks at Jordan, "and we both know who put him on to us."

Jordan, looking out at Brayden, "You have that right. I put Brayden on him and you know what he got out of him," he grins.

What next?

Jordan and Karen sit there on the beach watching Brayden out on the water kiteboarding.

Karen keeps looking forward towards Brayden, "so I wonder how much Rick told this Bill guy?"

Jordan, watching Brayden also; not wanting Bill to know that they know that he is watching them. "That's a good question. He did try to start asking some detailed questions, but that is when the trolley arrived. So, we told him that we had to go, and we did."

Karen looks Jordan's way, "you left him standing there?"

He grins, "Yes, we did."

"He must have followed you here," she says, as she looks back out at Brayden.

"Now we have two problems, Rick and Bill," Jordan says with a disgusting look. "I wonder what Tarke thinks about this?"

"That question you will have to ask him." she turns to Jordan, "it looks like Brayden is coming in."

"You are right; I'll go and see what he wants to do." Jordan stands and heads to the shoreline to see Brayden.

When Jordan reaches the shore, Brayden is already there. "Well, what do you think?" Jordan asks.

Brayden is tired but still musters up a smile. "We have a good one here. I had a blast, but it's time for a break."

"Give me the kite and I'll take care of it," Jordan says, as Brayden is more than happy to give it to him.

Brayden picks up the board as Jordan takes the kite up on the beach and lowers it to the ground. With the kite secure, they walk over to where Karen is sitting.

Karen, watching them as they sit down, "I watched the both of you out there; it looks like you had a ball."

Brayden now has a big smile, "I had a blast."

Jordan looks at Brayden, "don't look around. Bill is up in the parking lot watching us."

Brayden's smile disappears and gets ready to stand. "No. No, don't get up." Jordan quickly says, stopping Brayden.

Brayden looks at Jordan, "I just wanted to have a word with him."

Karen jumps into the conversation, "you don't want to stir anything up, Brayden. We are going to have to think about what we can do."

"Bring it to Tarke," Brayden replies.

Jordan looks over to Brayden, "Karen and I have discussed that. I will bring it to Tarke. I think our kiteboarding is done today; let's put things away."

"I agree. I don't feel like giving Bill a show." Brayden looks at Karen and Jordan, "He has seen his Aliens today. He can put that in his notes." Brayden smiles as he gets up.

With Karen's help, it didn't take long to pack up everything. They grabbed their stuff and walked over to the pavilion where Jordan and Brayden could change out of their wetsuits.

After changing, Brayden walks over to the side of the pavilion to see if Bill was still there. He comes back where Jordan and Karen are sitting, "I didn't see him; I hope that he gave up and left."

Karen stands, "it's been an interesting day. Your kiteboarding was fun to watch, and Bill has me thinking."

Jordan looks at Brayden, "it's time for us to head home, also. Is your phone handy to give the trolley a call?"

"It's time for me to head out. See you guys again soon." Karen smiles and walks off.

Brayden makes the call for the trolley, "they told me that the trolley is coming to pick someone else up here, also. We should head for the parking lot now."

The next day Jordan decides it's time to have a talk with Tarke. Jordan messages Tarke, *Good morning, Tarke. I plan on coming to the ship today. Do you have time for a meeting?*

Tarke answers, *I was going to message you shortly. Yes, we can meet anytime today. I have some information for you.*

I'm going to have breakfast and then I'll be on my way, Jordan replies.

Jordan walks into the kitchen to see his mother at the table with a cup of coffee and the newspaper.

"Good morning," he says, as he chooses a box of cereal. "I'm going to the ship today."

Mother looks up, "have a good day," she says, as she puts the paper down. "Who is this investigator, Bill?"

Jordan stops and puts the box of cereal down. "What? You met Bill?"

"Yes, he came to the door right after you and Brayden left for the beach yesterday," she says, as she takes a sip of her coffee.

Jordan, looking at his mother thinking, *she doesn't seem too worried about Bill's visit.* "Did he ask you a lot of questions?"

Jordan's mother smiling, "yes, he did. I remembered my promise to keep the secret." She takes another sip of coffee, "I gave him the Brayden treatment."

"The Brayden treatment?" he asks with a questioning look on his face.

Mother still smiling, "yes, you should try it sometime; it was fun. Brayden has treated us all with his questions and twisted humor."

"Mother, I can't believe that you would do that," Jordan says, as he wants to laugh.

Mother gets serious, "he sure did try to get something out of me."

Jordan walks around the table and gives his mother a hug. "Thanks, Mother, you did well."

With the information about Bill that he got from his mother; he had to go. He put a breakfast sandwich in the microwave for a minute, then summoned his Explorer. He ate his sandwich as he quickly headed up to the campsite for the Explorer. Twenty minutes later he was entering the main ship.

Jordan walks out of the bridge into the main corridor.

"Good morning," one of the crew members says as he is walking by.

"Good morning. Have you seen Tarke?" Jordan asks.

"I saw him in the leisure room," he answers.

"Thanks," Jordan replies, as he heads to the leisure room. He looks down the hallway and spots Tarke walking his way.

They meet, "hi, Tarke." Jordan says, as they both stop in the hallway. "So, we both have a meeting in mind for today," Tarke grins. "We must be starting to think alike. Let's go in the conference room," Tarke says, as they are standing in front of the conference room.

They walk in and take seats. Tarke, looking at Jordan. "If you don't mind, I want to call in Harec and Karen."

Jordan agrees, "that will be good; what I have to talk about should include the both of them."

Tarke messages Harec and Karen and looks at Jordan. "They will be here for a minute or two."

"Good. We have another problem that I need to talk about," Jordan informs Tarke.

Tarke, looking at Jordan, "I know, we will get into it when they get here."

Harec and Karen walk into the room together and take seats. Tarke watching them get seated, "thanks for your time. Jordan and I have a couple subjects to discuss."

Harec replies, "you have our attention." he says as he looks at Karen as she nods her head in a yes motion.

Tarke looks over to Jordan, "you can be first; go ahead."

Jordan looks around the conference room table. "We all know that I have been having a problem with Rick." He looks at Karen, "I believe that Rick has reported us to the UFO investigation organization. We now have Bill, one of their investigators, hounding us. Yesterday he arrived at my home and started asking me questions." He looks at Karen, "then later at the beach; he was there watching Karen, Brayden, and me." Jordan looks over to Tarke, "then this morning I found out from my mother Bill had questioned her yesterday, also."

Karen gives Jordan a questioning look, "your mother?"

Jordan smiles, "this is funny. My mother told me that she gave Bill the Brayden treatment."

Tarke, looking at Jordan with a big grin, "the Brayden treatment." He turns to Harec, "you did a great job with the mind changing program that you had Karen use on Jordan's parents."

Harec smiling, "thanks, Tarke, I do my best."

Karen looks at Jordan, "we have a new term, Brayden treatment. That is good; I can only imagine what the Brayden treatment is."

Jordan is now half laughing, "Mother told me that with every question that Bill asked; she turned it into another question. And she would often change the subject. Bill didn't get anything from her. Mom was even smiling when she told me about her meeting with Bill." Jordan sits back for a minute, then looks back to Tarke. "My question is this. We have a problem; do you have any suggestions?"

Tarke sits back and looks around the table, then back to Jordan. "Jordan," he pauses a second looking at him. "You have all the tools that I have." He looks Jordan in the eyes. "You also have the knowledge. Think back in our past, how did we handle similar situations?" Tarke looks around the table again, "Jordan is in training to be in command of his own ship." He looks back at Jordan, "you have my full support, Jordan. How you handle this problem is totally up to you." Tarke looks at Harec and Karen, "Jordan is second in command of this ship; his wish is your command."

Jordan sits back remembering; *I have been so busy with other things that I haven't been thinking about my training and my position.* "Yes, Tarke, I have been taking a break and need to get back on track." He looks at Tarke, "I'm on it." Jordan looks at Karen, and she gives him a, thumbs up.

Tarke looks at Harec, "I have some good news." He turns to Jordan, "remember Brayden's suggestion?"

Jordan puts his mind back on track. "The watch transmitter idea?"

Tarke smiles, "yes, his idea has been approved by the elders." He looks back to Harec, "they are in production, and with the ease and security in mind they also have redesigned the medallion to half of its size."

Harec replies, "that is great! It took Brayden to bring up the good idea with the watch. Now look where that took us; when will they be available?"

"They will be on the next supply ship," Tarke replies.

Jordan looks at everyone, "I'm not going to tell Brayden until they arrive."

Karen looks at Jordan, "let's plan a special surprise occasion for the unveiling."

Jordan smiles, "let me think about it. I have a great idea already." Jordan thinks a secret message to Tarke. Tarke looks at Jordan and nods his head in a yes motion.

Time with Grandpa

Jordan is relaxing on the front porch listening to the radio when Mother opens up the front door. "Brayden is on the phone," she says as she hands him his phone.

He takes the phone, "hi, Brayden, what's up?"

"I was wondering if you want to go and visit Grandpa and Grandma?" he asks.

Jordan quickly replies, "why, yes, that sounds like a good idea. I was just sitting here on the front porch listening to the radio and doing some thinking."

"I'll hop on my bike and shoot your way. See you in a short," and Brayden hangs up the phone.

Jordan puts his phone down and leans back in his chair. It didn't take long for Brayden to come riding in the driveway. He parks his bike by the garage and walks to the front porch.

He looks at Jordan relaxing, "tough life today," he says as he takes a seat.

Jordan smiles, "yep; someone has to do it."

"So, what have you been thinking about?" Brayden asks.

Jordan looks over at Brayden, "Rick and Bill; must I say anymore?"

"Nope, say no more. We need to go for our visit and relax your brain," says Brayden, as he gets up from his chair and stands there looking at Jordan.

Jordan turns off the radio and grabs his phone. "Let's go," he says as he gets up from his seat.

Jordan pops the front door open and sticks his head in, "Mom, Brayden and I are going to Grandpa's and Grandma's house."

She replies, "thanks for telling me; have a good time."

They go back to the garage where Jordan opens up the door and gets his bike. Fifteen minutes later they are riding up Grandpa's driveway to their house. As they get close to the house, they hear a car horn.

Jordan looks around behind him to see Grandpa in his car behind them. "It's Grandpa coming," he tells Brayden.

They ride to the side of the driveway to give Grandpa room to drive by.

Grandpa slows down and stops along the side of them, then opens up his window. "I didn't notice that it was you two until I passed you. So, I turned around; I was heading to the marina to take a boat ride. Do you two want to go with me?"

Jordan looks at Brayden, "I do; how about you?"

Brayden quickly answers, "yes, let's go."

Jordan looking in the window of the car, "we would love to go. We are going to park our bikes by the garage."

Grandpa replies, "I'll meet you there."

They ride to the garage and park their bikes and hop into Grandpa's car. Grandpa heads around and out of the driveway and off to the marina.

Brayden looks at Grandpa, "we didn't stop in and say hi to Grandmother."

"I'll give her a call to tell her what happened," Grandpa tells him.

"We will spend time with her later today," Jordan adds.

They arrive at the marina and with help from Jordan and Brayden, they were on the way out to Lake Michigan. Grandpa and Brayden are in the cabin talking as they go through the channel. Jordan has found his spot in the back of the boat, stretched out on a seat enjoying the ride. After around fifteen minute's Grandpa walks to the back of the boat and takes a seat next to Jordan.

"Brayden is having fun driving the boat," he says, as he leans back in his seat. "What are you thinking?" Grandpa asks as he looks at Jordan. "You have been quite in your own world today."

Jordan looks at Grandpa, "I had a meeting with Tarke about Rick and Bill."

"Bill?" grandpa asks, looking puzzled.

"Oh, I haven't told you about Bill." Jordan sits up. "We believe that Rick has reported his seeing the Explorer to the UFO reporting agency or organization, whatever it is. Bill is one of their investigators."

Grandpa sits up also, "investigator. So, I take it that Bill has paid you a visit."

Jordan looks forward, "yes, he has. He also had a talk with Mother. Then I spotted him using a pair of binoculars watching Karen, Brayden and me at the beach.

"Bill is on a mission; he must have been convinced that you know something," Grandpa replies with a questioning look on his face. "What did Tarke have to say about it?"

Jordan looks at Grandpa, "what he told me is what has me thinking." He looks out at the lake then back to Grandpa, "Tarke reminded me that I'm now second in command. He told me that it's up to me to deal with Rick and Bill. He told me that I have all the powers that he has and I have all the knowledge of previous similar situations. I have his full support."

Grandpa, looking at Jordan, "that is good! Remember how quickly you handled Rick in the sporting goods store." Grandpa stands and looks at the boat cabin where Brayden is in control. "How much does Brayden know?"

Jordan looks up at Grandpa, "I told him a little bit. That's when he said, let's go to Grandpa's and Grandmother's house. He was trying to get my mind off of everything." He looks towards Brayden, as he is having fun at the steering wheel. "It's okay; I'm not worried about Rick and Bill. I know that I have the ability to take care of them and the problem."

Grandpa looks back at Jordan, "good; it's good to hear that you are confident in your abilities."

Brayden shuts the motor of the boat off and walks back to where Grandpa and Jordan are now sitting.

Brayden looks at them, "I think that we are out far enough." He sits down, "it looked like you two were having a good conversation."

"Yes, we were. I was telling Grandpa about our new friend, Bill," Jordan tells Brayden with a half grin.

Brayden smiles, "I gave him the run around the other day when he stopped over to Jordan's house."

Jordan, looking at Brayden, "at my meeting with Tarke we decided to call your so-called run around the Brayden treatment." He smiles, "Karen came up with that. We all thought that was a good idea, and even Tarke had a smile. I know that he is remembering how you grilled him when you two first met."

"Let's get back to Rick and Bill. What are you going to do if they get in your face, zap them?" Brayden asks, knowing that Jordan can zap them good.

"No, Brayden, I'm not sure what I'm going to do. Right now, I'm going to watch them for a while and see what they are going to do or try."

Grandpa is just sitting there listing to Jordan's answers. "Good idea, Jordan; good idea."

Grandpa looks at Brayden, "I have some pop in the cooler if you want some."

Brayden gets up and heads to the cooler, "I'll take one. How about you guys?"

They both say yes and Brayden brings back pops for them. They sit there on the boat talking and enjoy the gentle rocking of the boat in the Lake Michigan waves.

Later that day, they are sitting on the lakeside porch with Grandmother and Grandpa. Grandmother had made a fresh batch of cookies and a pitcher of ice cold lemonade that they are enjoying. Grandmother had her knitting out showing everything off to Jordan and Brayden. They both had a pile of knitted items that they were told to take home to their mothers.

It was a good day for Jordan that had relaxed his thinking. Brayden had a good idea when he suggested that they spend the day with Grandpa and Grandmother.

They both headed back home before it got dark.

The message

Rick is lying on his couch with a photography magazine when he hears knocking on his front door. He gets up and walks to the door and opens it to see Bill standing there.

"Hi, Bill; you have news for me?" Rick asks.

"May I come in? I have a few Items that I want to discuss with you," Bill replies.

Rick, looking at Bill thinking, *what does this dude want now?* "Sure, let's have a seat at the table."

They walk over to the table and take seats. Bill opens up his briefcase and takes out a tablet.

He looks at a few pages in his tablet, then looks up. "You told me about your friend, Jordan, being associated with Aliens." He glances down at his tablet, "I had a talk with a fellow called Brayden. I couldn't get anything from him; then I tried Jordan with no results."

Rick gives Bill a disgusting look, "did you think that they would spill the beans with you?"

"Well, sometimes it's worth a try. I didn't get anything out of Jordan's mother either," Bill explains.

Rick looking at Bill, "you are dealing with Aliens." He puts his hands out in front of him in a questioning motion. "I don't know if you have ever dealt with Aliens before. They are crafty!"

Bill looks at his notes again. "I saw Jordan and Brayden at the beach with alien green wetsuits on," he says as he looks up to Rick. "Are you sure that isn't what you saw?"

That question upset Rick and he pounds the table. "No! I saw a UFO with an Alien coming out of it." Rick holds back not wanting Bill to walk out. "I had pictures, but they somehow were able to destroy them.

Bill thinking, *boy, they have upset him. I bet he has done more than what he is telling me.* "Okay, Rick, I believe you. If there is any more that you have to share with me, please do."

"Bill, I have given you everything that I know," Rick tells Bill, as he holds back the full truth.

Bill closes his tablet and looks at Rick. "Let me talk with my colleagues and figure out a way to get to the bottom of this."

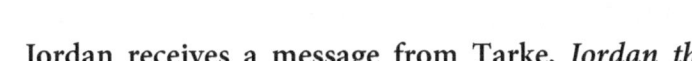

Jordan receives a message from Tarke, *Jordan the new transmitters have arrived. I have made the arrangement for your surprise. How does tomorrow afternoon sound?*

Jordan smiles, *perfect; I'll be in touch with you tomorrow. Let's do this; Brayden can use a good surprise.*

Tarke messages, *okay, I'll make the arrangements. I have to say this is going to be fun.*

Jordan picks up his phone and gives Brayden a call. "Hi, Brayden, I was wondering if you want to go camping tomorrow?"

"Tomorrow, that's Wednesday?" Brayden responds.

Jordan thinks quickly, "yep, it's Wednesday. I figure Rick always hits us on the weekend."

"Good thinking. Yes, Wednesday is okay with me. I'm in for camping tomorrow. Want me to bring anything?" Brayden asks.

Jordan is thinking that they will not need anything tomorrow. "Nope, I have it covered. How about we get together tomorrow early afternoon?"

Brayden responds, "okay, I'll be over at twelve thirty."

Jordan is thinking, *that's Brayden.* "No, around two will be fine. We can clean up the camp area then use Dad's tractor to take everything up."

"Okay, two o'clock; clean up, then set up. I'll see you tomorrow." Brayden hangs up the phone.

Jordan lays back down on his bed thinking; *this is going to be a good time.*

Later in the afternoon, Jordan hops on his bike to ride over to see Grandpa. On his way, he is thinking, *here I am on my bicycle peddling my way to Grandpa's house. I don't have a car and even a driver's license, but I have a UFO. I can fly my Explorer anywhere around this world.* Jordan stops for a couple minutes looking around and down at his bike thinking to himself. *Actually, this is really nice, it keeps my life as I know it.* He pushes off and continues on his way. A couple minutes later he is riding up to Grandpa's and Grandmother's house. After parking his bike, he walks to the door and gives it his usual two knocks, then walks in.

Grandmother comes walking out of the kitchen. "Hi, Jordan, he's down in his man's room," she says with a smile.

Jordan grins, knowing that this is just Grandmother. "That doesn't surprise me," he replies, looking at Grandmother. "I don't smell any cooking going on."

"Not yet; I was looking through my recipes for something good to make," she answers.

"I'll let you get back to your searching. Love you, Grandma."

"I love you too, Jordy," Grandmother replies as she heads back into the kitchen.

Jordan heads down to the man's room. This time he is going to turn things around. Jordan messages Grandpa, *I'm coming down to give you a visit.* He walks over and opens up the door.

Grandpa is sitting there watching him walk in. "You got me this time," he says, watching Jordan come in and take a seat.

Jordan gets comfortable and looks at Grandpa with a grin. "Have you heard anything from Tarke lately?"

Grandpa replies, "no, not in a few days. Why, what's up?"

"I have what I want to share with you." Jordan pulls out his medallion from around his neck, "remember Brayden's idea about making a transceiver style watch?"

"You're going to tell me that it has been approved?" Grandpa asks, as he looks at Jordan's medallion.

Jordan is sitting there beaming with excitement. "Yes, they have! And, with Brayden's suggestion, they have redesigned the medallion to half this size." Jordan is showing his medallion to Grandpa.

Grandpa feels his medallion under his shirt. "Smaller is good, but also in a watch style; that's awesome!"

Jordan is now sitting there with a huge smile, "that's amazing, and Brayden doesn't know about it yet."

Grandpa's eyes open wide as he looks at Jordan, "you have something planned, don't you?"

Jordan can't sit anymore and gets up, feeling excited. "Yes, I do! That is why I came over here," he turns to Grandpa. Tarke has the new transmitters, and I have special plans for tomorrow. I would like you to be on the ship by seven tomorrow. Can you do that?"

Grandpa watching Jordan pacing around, "I wouldn't miss it for anything." He smiles, "you have something good planned; I can see that in your actions."

"Oh, yes, I do!" Jordan sits back down, trying to calm himself down. "I had a talk with Tarke about Rick and Bill. To make it short, Tarke told me that how they are handled is totally up to me. He said that I have the knowledge and the powers to take care of their potential problems."

Grandpa replies, "Jordan, I have had some talks with Tarke, and he likes how you handle situations that pop up. I'm sure that you have his full support."

"Yes, Grandpa, that is what he told me." Jordan smiles and sits back in his chair.

Brayden's arrives

It's Tuesday and Jordan is anticipating his surprise that he has planned for Brayden. He has messaged Tarke in the preparation of what will be happening. Tarke has everything on his side of the big day for Brayden arranged. Jordan also messaged Pete and Karen and disguised his plans with them. Everything is going to be something very special for the unveiling of Brayden's suggested transmitter watches. Now it's just waiting for Brayden to arrive.

Jordan is sitting in the living room with his mother telling her about his plans for today.

Jordan looks out of the front window to see Brayden coming into the driveway on his bike. "Here he comes, mums the word."

Mother smiles, "I got you, I won't say a thing." She stands up to go to the door, "have fun, I'll let him in."

Jordan turns the TV volume up a little, so it looks like he is just watching TV.

Brayden walks into the living room, "Mom told me that you were in here. Is there a good show on?" he asks.

Jordan looks over at Brayden, "no, not really. I'm just sitting here thinking."

Brayden takes a seat on the couch, "yeah, let's not think about those two bozos today."

Jordan looks at the clock on the wall; it's exactly two o'clock. "Boy, when you say that you will be over around two, you weren't kidding."

He looks at Jordan, "I think that the both of us need a nice quiet peaceful camping night."

Jordan looks at the TV, not wanting to show any emotions as he is thinking. *Boy if he knew what is in store for him this afternoon.* "Yep, that's what I was thinking," Jordan says in a normal sounding voice.

Brayden still looking at Jordan, "let's go out and at least get the camping stuff out."

Jordan stands up thinking; *that's a good idea. It will take my mind off of things a little.* "Let's go."

Brayden gets up, and they both head to the garage where all the camping equipment is.

They walk by Jordan's mother, "you two have a good camp night. I'll make up a food basket later." Mother mentioned the food basket so Brayden wouldn't worry about it. Jordan and she had talked about the surprise and decided there would be no need for it.

They go into the garage and start getting everything out and putting it on the backyard picnic table. Jordan is taking his time, knowing that they have around four and a half hours before his plan is to start.

Jordan puts a couple camping chairs down on the table. He looks at Brayden as he comes with the sleeping bags. "Hey, I forgot about something for lunch. Let's go grab something," he says, knowing that Brayden wouldn't pass up something to eat.

"Yes, let's go grab something," Brayden replies as he sets the sleeping bags down.

They head into the house and take a look in the refrigerator.

Jordan looks at Brayden, "we had ham the other day. Let's make a couple ham sandwiches" he says as he takes the dish of ham out.

They make their sandwiches and have a glass of milk. Jordan's mother walks into the kitchen dining area. "Good, I'm glad you came in to get something to eat."

Brayden looks over to mother, "we made ham sandwiches, and they are good," he says, as he takes his last bite.

She smiles, "good, that should hold you until supper time." Jordan's mother walks out of the room with a grin on her face trying to get out before she spills the beans.

Jordan looks up at the clock and can see that they had used up a good amount of time. He finishes his sandwich and glass of milk, "why don't you get the rest of the stuff out and I'll gas up the tractor and hook up the trailer."

Brayden gets up and puts his plate and glass in the dishwasher. "Okay, I'll catch you out at the table," and he heads out of the house.

Jordan takes care of his stuff and walks into the living room to find his mother. "Thanks, you handled that well. We will have a good time; I'll tell you about it tomorrow," then he walks out to get the tractor ready to take everything up to the campsite. Jordan takes his time getting the tractor ready, then drives it around to the picnic table where Brayden is waiting for him.

Brayden looks at Jordan, "what did you have to do, drill for gas?" he says with a smile.

Jordan gets off of the tractor, "no, I forgot where to put the gas," he says making a joke.

Brayden looks at the trailer, then at the pile of camping stuff. "I bet we can get everything in the trailer."

Jordan looks everything over, "it's a good possibility."

They get to work packing everything. With a little arranging, they are packed and ready to go to the campsite. With Brayden following Jordan on the tractor, up to the campsite they go.

They arrive up to the camping area, and Jordan gets off of the tractor. "Here we go, let's get this thing unloaded," Jordan says, as he is waiting for a comment from Brayden because he drove so slow. But nothing was said as he unloads the trailer. Jordan quickly looks at his phone to see what time it is. It's now four-thirty; he has used up enough time so they can get the camp set up at a normal pace.

They both work together to get the tent up. Then they split up and do their usual jobs getting the camp ready for the night.

Brayden is the first one to sit down, "we did good; that only took an hour."

Jordan pulls out his phone and looks at it, "you're right, I have to take Dad's tractor back. Do you want to come along or try to make the fire?"

Brayden hops on the challenge, "try to make a fire. You make it sound like I don't know how to make a fire. You're on. I'll have a roaring fire by the time you get back."

Jordan replies with a smile, "roaring?"

"Yes, roaring. And bring up the food basket if you can without the tractor," Brayden puts in his reply with a grin.

Jordan gets on the tractor and heads back down to the house. Brayden acts as if he is in no hurry until Jordan is out of sight. Then he quickly starts picking out the wood for the fire.

A half hour later Jordan comes walking back into the campsite.

Brayden looks at him, "where is the food basket?"

Jordan comes out with his excuse, "Mom is working on it and told me that it won't be ready until around seven-thirty or eight."

Brayden grins, "she must be making us something really good."

Jordan sits down, "well, Brayden, you do have a roaring fire; this is nice," he says, as he leans his seat back and looks up at the sky thinking. *Only an hour to go.*

The surprise

They have been sitting at the fire talking about the good old times when they would go at each other about UFOs and Aliens. They were having a good time when Jordan receives a message from Pete. *Harec and Karen are above you and I have your Explorer alongside them.*

Jordan grins as he messages back, *okay, Pete, in the tent now.* Jordan looks over to Brayden, "I have something in the tent that I want to show you. I'll go and get it.

Jordan walks over to the tent and goes in. When he is in the tent, there is Pete. "Hi, Pete, are you ready for this?"

Pete replies, "we all are ready."

Brayden turns, hearing talking, "what, are you talking to yourself?" he yells.

He doesn't get a reply from Jordan. Brayden is now wondering what Jordan is doing, so he gets up from his chair.

Pete looks at Jordan, "there is nothing to be scared of; transportation is safe. Your Explorer is waiting for you."

Jordan smiles, "okay here I go." Jordan quickly fades out of sight.

Pete can hear footsteps coming towards the tent, so he steps out. Brayden stops, looking at Pete, "where did you come from?"

"The tent," Pete replies, as he gives Brayden a questioning look.

Brayden, looking at Pete, "so you are what Jordan went in the tent for?"

Pete replies, "Jordan? I didn't see Jordan in the tent."

"Okay, you guys, that's good; you got me." and he looks in the tent, to find out that Jordan is not there.

Brayden turns to Pete, "I saw him go into the tent, what did you do with him?" he smiles, "funny."

All of a sudden Brayden notices someone sitting in Jordan's camp chair. "Okay, I see him," he walks over to the campfire to see it's not Jordan sitting there. "Karen, what's going on?" he says as he looks at Karen, then Pete. "I thought that tonight was going to be a good old camping night."

Karen gets up from her seat, "well, Brayden, tonight is a special night."

Pete, smiling as he looks at Brayden, "come over here." Brayden walks over by Pete.

"Okay, what's so special?" he asks.

Pete, looking at Brayden, "look up, do you see the Explorer?"

Brayden looks at Pete then looks up to the sky, "no, it's invisible."

Pete looks at Brayden, "you soon will."

Things go black then all of a sudden, he is in the Explorer with Jordan. He looks around, "dang, I transported!" He looks at Jordan, "they told me that this was going to be a special night. I transported. That's special."

"Yes, you sure did. I transported for the first time a little while ago myself," answered Jordan. "I have more for you tonight."

"What about the campfire?" Brayden asks.

Jordan, looking at Brayden as he is smiling, "don't worry; Karen and Pete will take care of it."

Brayden comes back with another question, "so, how about our food basket?"

"Brayden, sit down," Jordan tells Brayden. "Mother isn't making a food basket."

Jordan starts laughing, "come on, Brayden. You just got transported and all you are thinking about is the food basket."

Brayden realizes what he was asking and smiles. "I just didn't want Mom to make the basket of food for nothing."

Jordan decides to tell Brayden just a little bit of what is going on. "I had this planned and Mother knew everything. She never was going to make a food basket." Jordan positions himself to control the Explorer. "Karen and Pete are going to take the camp down and put everything away."

Brayden looks at Jordan, "they don't have the tractor."

Jordan smiles. Brayden thinks about it; they have their ways.

Brayden sits back, "yeah, I know. So, what are we going to do now?"

"We are going to stay the night on the ship. You have said that it would be fun. Well, here is your chance." Jordan takes control of the Explorer and off they go.

Brayden looks out of the Explorer as they head out over the lake. "And you had this all planned; you're getting pretty sneaky. I'm going to have to keep an eye on you."

They fly out over Lake Michigan then sink down into the water. Slowly the main ship comes into view; Jordan messages Tarke. *We are about to dock; Brayden knows nothing.*

Tarke replies, *I'll be waiting for you at the bridge door.*

The messaging ends as Jordan brings the Explorer to a stop at the docking station.

Jordan looks at Brayden as he is feeling full of anticipation. Then he opens the hatch, "I'm following you." Out they go through the bridge way. Brayden, looking forward can see Tarke standing there waiting for them.

Brayden looks at Jordan, "Tarke's waiting for us."

Jordan can't hold back anymore, "no, Brayden, he's waiting for you," he says with a big smile.

They walk out of the bridge to see not only Tarke but half of the crew standing there.

"Brayden, Brayden, Brayden," they are chanting.

Brayden gives Jordan a questioning look as Jordan smiles back.

Tarke stops Brayden by putting his hand on his shoulder. "This is a special day for everyone, and it's because of you."

Brayden looks at him, "me?" he gets out with a stunned look.

Tarke looking at Brayden, "come with me."

They start walking down the hallway. All Brayden can think is remembering Jordan's walk like this. He starts to

165

think. *No, I'm not an Alien. Also, I wasn't adopted. Are my parents Aliens and I don't know?* Questions and crazy thoughts keep going through his head as they head down the hallway.

Tarke stops by the conference room door, "Brayden I want to be the first one to say thank you," and he reaches out to shake Brayden's hand. Brayden shakes Tarke's hand, still wondering what is going on.

Jordan steps forward, "Brayden, I arranged this for you. Let's go in so your questions can be answered. I was listening to your thoughts as we were walking here. No, you are not an Alien, I want to get that out right away." He smiles at Brayden, "but on the other hand, maybe you should be."

They walk into the conference room to first see the Elders standing there waiting for them.

Jordan walks Brayden up to the Elders, "Brayden, this is Zen."

Zen replies, "I'm sure you remember me. H̲i, Brayden."

Jordan turns to the next Elder, "Brayden, this is Arn."

Arn nods his head, "nice to meet you again, Brayden."

They take another step over, "and this is Raymoth."

Raymoth smiles, "good afternoon, Brayden."

Brayden looks around the room and spots Grandpa sitting at the conference room table. Next to Grandpa is who but Karen and Pete sitting there with huge smiles. The room is full of ranking crew members, watching them enter the room.

Brayden can only stand there in total amazement thinking, *what the heck did I do to deserve this?*

The presentation

Brayden stands back a step, looking at the Elders, "I don't know what I did to deserve this greeting," he says. "It's my pleasure to meet you again," he says to the Elders.

Zen looks over to Jordan, "this is your meeting." He looks at the other Elders, and they step back a few steps. Zen looks at Jordan, "Jordan you may begin."

Jordan looks at Zen than to Tarke. Tarke nods his head as if to say, go ahead. Jordan looks at Brayden, "follow me." They walk over to the head of the table. With Brayden by his side, Jordan, using his ship commanding powers, turns on the ship-wide speakers so all the crew can hear what he is about to say.

Jordan smiles as he looks at Brayden, "well, buddy, this is your day." He looks around the table, "hello, crew, this is Jordan Kingston. As some may know, we are having a meeting and I have some information that I would like to share with you." Jordan looks at Brayden, "Brayden, do you remember your suggestion that you made to Tarke, a few weeks ago?"

Brayden thinks for a moment, "are you talking about the watch thing?"

Jordan looks at Tarke then back to Brayden, "yes, Brayden. the watch thing." Jordan looks at the Elders, "your watch transceiver idea has been approved."

Everyone on the ship has full attention to what they are hearing. Jordan continues, "not only has the watch style transceiver been approved, but they have also redesigned the transceiver medallion to half its present size."

Everyone in the conference room is looking at Jordan wondering what else he has to tell them.

Jordan looks around the room, "the watch and the new medallions have been made and are here for everyone."

Brayden looks around with the biggest smile now knowing that his suggestions were taken.

Jordan looks at Harec, "Harec, please come up here and present Brayden the first set of new transceivers."

Tarke has been sitting there watching and listening to Jordan as he is conducting the meeting, in full compliance with how Jordan is handling himself.

Harec walks over to Brayden with two small boxes and hands them to Jordan. Jordan takes the boxes with a smile. He looks at Brayden, "you get the first set of transceivers, Brayden. I haven't even seen them yet," and he hands the boxes to Brayden.

Brayden, gleaming with pride, opens up the first box to see the small medallion. "Wow, the new small medallion is cool. It won't be so bulky wearing it." He opens up the second box. He looks at the Elders, "this watch medallion is boss. Thank you for using my idea." Brayden can't wait and puts the watch on.

Jordan speaks a message to the crew, "I will be personally meeting with each one of the crew and presenting you with the new transceivers. Have a good day." And Jordan turns off the speakers in the ship.

Brayden is standing there next to Jordan wanting to do the happy dance with joy.

Jordan looks at Tarke, "my part of the meeting is over, the rest, if anything, is up to you." Jordan smiles at Brayden and walks over by Grandpa and takes a seat.

Brayden, watching Jordan walk away, now wonders, *what is going to happen now?*

Tarke stands and walks over to Brayden. "Brayden, you are a smart, talented young man." Tarke receives a message from Zen, *Tarke I would like to have a talk with you.* Tarke looks at Brayden, "just one minute." Tarke walks over to the Elders, and they step back and circle in a group and have a short discussion. Tarke nods his head and walks back to Brayden.

Brayden is standing there now wondering, *now what's up?*

Tarke stands next to Brayden, then looks out to the people around the conference room table. "Something special has been declared." Tarke looks at Brayden, "this is a first for me!" he says making a statement, "it has been decided that you Brayden have been totally accepted into our community." Tarke looks over to Jordan and his grandfather, then back to Brayden. "It has been suggested by the Elders that you be allowed to go through our learning sessions. Only a few special humans in the past have been given this opportunity."

Brayden looks over to the Elders, "thank you."

The Elders look at each other and then walk up to Brayden. Zen the head Elder puts his hand on Brayden's back, seeing that he is getting emotional. "Brayden, we have been watching you." Zen smiles, "I like you and your humor, but most of all, your imagination and thirst for knowledge." He pats Brayden on the back. Zen looks at Tarke, then out at Harec. "Harec, we will give Tarke our orders for Brayden's sessions before we leave." Zen looks at the other two Elders, "Arn, you have something that you want to tell Jordan." Arn steps forward, looking at Jordan. "Jordan, you have been taught well," he puts his hand up to his head. "Believe, believe in yourself." Arn's thoughts go directly to Jordan. *We have been watching you also, Jordan. You are doing well; you have the knowledge and skills to handle any problem. Believe.*

Jordan smiles and nods his head in a yes motion to Arn thinking back. *Yes, I do believe Arn. Thanks for messaging me and not taking anything away from Brayden's day.*

Arn steps back and then Raymoth steps forward. "I have to say; we enjoy our visits. We always have a good discussion about our time on your ship." Raymoth looks over to Brayden with a grin, knowing that he is going to like what he is about to say. "Our people will welcome you with open arms when you make your visit to our world."

Brayden looking at Raymoth, "I'm ready now! Do you have room for a hitchhiker?" he asks with a big smile.

Zen speaks up, "not today, Brayden; your day is coming."

Tarke, knowing that the Elders are scheduled to leave soon, jumps into the conversation. "Brayden, are you ready to spend the night here?"

Brayden smiles, "yes, and for supper."

Jordan stands, "I think that our meeting is over. Thank you, Zen, Arn, and Raymoth for coming."

Grandpa has been sitting there quietly enjoying watching his two grandsons. All his dreams and hopes are coming true before his eyes. He has been choked up with pride and holding back his tears of joy. Tarke and the Elders leave the conference room as Jordan heads over to see Brayden.

Brayden hands the box with the watch transmitter in it to Jordan. "Take a look at this; it's nice," he says with a big grin.

Jordan takes the transmitter out of the box, "this is nice. I haven't seen one until now." He holds it over his wrist, "who would ever know. Show me the medallion." He puts the transmitter back in the box, as Brayden hands him the other box. Jordan opens the box, "yes, much nicer," he says as he looks the new smaller medallion over.

They hadn't noticed that there is a crowd gathering around them.

Grandpa, looking at Jordan and Brayden, "good job. You two are going to make everyone on the ship happy.

Jordan thinks for a couple minutes as Brayden shows the two new transmitters to everyone. "Brayden, tomorrow you will help me hand these out to everyone."

"That will be fun," Brayden replies.

Jordan answers, "it was your idea, and it's you that should actually hand them out."

Grandpa looks at Jordan smiling, "Jordan that is nice of you to give that option to Brayden."

Jordan steps back as everybody starts leaving the room and stopping to say something to Brayden. Around fifteen minutes later the room was almost empty. The only people left were Grandpa, Pete, Karen, and Jordan. Brayden looks at them, "it's time to eat."

With smiles, they all head to the lunch room.

The next day

Tarke and the Elders go into Tarke's office to have a talk before they leave.

Zen looks at the others, "we had a discussion about Brayden; and came to an agreement that he will be a real asset to us."

Tarke replies, "I agree, he is always thinking and asking questions."

"Brayden is going to be our knowledge bridge with the humans," says Raymoth.

Arn looks at Tarke, "we will give Harec our directives for Brayden's learning sessions before we leave."

Tarke grins as he looks at the Elders, "you know that this is going to be an interesting challenge. I'm going to have to keep a close eye on him."

Zen smiles, "you have Jordan. Between both of you, everything will be fine," he tells Tarke. "We have to see Harec, then we will be off."

Raymoth looks at Tarke, "we will be waiting for your reports," he says as he turns to leave Tarke's office.

The next day Brayden wakes up in his bed on the ship. He looks around and Jordan is already up and gone somewhere. He gets up and gets ready for his day of passing out the new transmitters. The first thing that is going through his mind is breakfast, so he heads to the lunch room. Upon entering the lunch room, he spots Jordan and Pete sitting there talking.

Brayden walks up to them and takes a seat. "How long have you been up?" he asks Jordan.

"Not long. I came here and met up with Pete and we were just talking about yesterday."

Brayden smiles, "wasn't that something!" He looks at Jordan, "you got one on me that time."

Pete looks at Brayden, "that's one time that you were speechless." He smiles. "We don't see that often."

Jordan reaches over and pats Brayden on the back. "You handled it very well."

"Yes, you did," Pete replies.

Brayden turns to Jordan, "today is the big day. We get to pass out the transmitters." He looks over at the food display, "but I'm hungry."

"Go get your breakfast. Pete and I will be behind you."

They have their breakfast as they have a good talk about yesterday and Jordan having the Elders come for the celebration. Brayden was wondering how the learning sessions work. Jordan had told him about his learning sessions, but now it would be his turn. This is going to be something that is going to be running through Brayden's head until his first session happens. They finish their breakfast and Pete has to go report in for duty.

Pete walks out, then Jordan looks back to Brayden, "let's go to see Harec and get the transmitters."

They both get up and take care of their breakfast utensils and head to see Harec.

They walk into Harec's medical room. Harec is seated by his control center as they walk up to him.

"Good morning, Harec, we came to pick up the transmitters," says Jordan.

Harec turns back to Jordan and Brayden, "where are you going to pass them out?"

"In the conference room; that will be a good central location," Jordan answers.

Harec stands and walks over to a bunch of metal containers. "You don't want to carry these; I'll transport them to the conference room. They will be there when you get there."

Brayden smiles, thinking, *This is too cool. Wouldn't it be cool to transport our camping gear up to the campsite?* He, all of a sudden, receives a message, *how do you think Karen and Pete took the camp down so fast yesterday?* Brayden smiles back at Jordan.

They walk back to the conference room to see the containers sitting there neatly.

Brayden looks at the two containers, "they got here before we did. Transportation is too cool."

"Well, Brayden, the watch transmitters were your idea." Jordan looks at Brayden, "so why don't you pass them out and I'll pass out the new medallions."

They open the containers and, by luck, Brayden opened up the watch transmitters. Brayden has his on. It was the first thing that he did when he woke up.

Jordan gets a message from Harec. *Jordan, I forgot to mention that you have to collect the old medallions.*

Jordan replies, *we will do that and turn them in to you when we are done.*

Harec messages back, *once they receive their new transmitters and before they turn in the old transmitter, they have to message me so I can sync the new ones to them. I'm sorry that I didn't let you know when you were here earlier.*

Jordan replies, *that's okay, I know now before we start passing them out.*

Jordan tells Brayden what Harec just told him in his messages. Jordan makes a shipwide announcement letting the crew know; that on their breaks they can pick up the new transmitters. Jordan and Brayden prepare for a fun day, as each one of the crew members stops by.

It was a long day as all the crew members stopped in to claim their new transmitters. Brayden received a thank you and praise from everyone. It was so much fun that his face hurt at the end of the day from smiling.

Jordan sits back in his seat in the conference room. He looks down at all the old medallion transmitters in one of the boxes. "It's almost eight o'clock."

"Yes, and my parents are going to wonder where I'm at," Brayden says, as his smile turns into a questioning look.

Jordan looks over to Brayden, "one good thing; my parents are now believers and know where we are." He looks around, "I'll call my mother and have her call and tell your mother that we are going to camp another night."

"So we can stay here another night?" Brayden asks as he cracks a small smile.

Jordan smiles as he looks at Brayden, "yes, another night."

It was another good time on the ship as they talked to the crew members as they stopped by the leisure room. They had a short talk with Tarke in the morning before they boarded Jordan's Explorer and headed back home.

Thinking

Rick hears a knock on his door. He walks over and opens up the door to see Bill standing there. "Hi, Rick, may I come in? I have something to talk to you about."

Rick answers, "Yes. Come on in," he says, as he has been wondering if or when Bill would show his face here again.

Bill walks in now with two briefcases, one in each hand. "We have been talking about you and your situation in the office. Let's take a seat; I would like to show you some things."

Rick is happy to see Bill and says, "Sure," wondering what he has to show him.

They take their seats at Rick's table and Bill puts his briefcases on the table. Looking over to Rick, "we may have a plan." He opens up one of his briefcases and takes out a small light brown object. "This is an undercover spy style micro-motion detection video camera." He hands it to Rick.

Rick takes it and looks it over, "this is cool." The camera is a little smaller than a deck of cards. He can see that it has been repainted a light brown, the same color as the sticks out in the woods.

Bill looking at Rick, "we have put in a large capacity microchip. With a full charge, it will record an hour of video," he says with a grin.

Rick, looking at the camera, then up at Bill, "but they always know somehow that I'm around their camp."

Bill replies, "Yes, we talked about that." He reaches into the briefcase again and pulls out a handheld GPS. He shows it to Rick, "do you know how to use this?" he asks.

"I sure do; I have one just like this," Rick replies.

Bill smiles, "good, then you don't need this one." He puts it on the table, "this is what we came up with." Bill looks up at Rick, "I don't know where the campsite is. We want you to just casually walk to the sight and mark the coordinates with your GPS. Then give me a call and let me know what they are."

"Then you are going to hide the cameras?" he asks.

"Not me, they know me. We have another quite sneaky investigator that will hide a few of these around the camp area." Bill says with a smile as he is holding one of the small micro cameras.

Rick wasn't sure if he liked Bill, but he now is starting to like his thinking. "I'll have the coordinates for you tomorrow," he says with a big grin on his face. *We will get those suckers,* Rick is thinking.

Bill puts everything back in his briefcase and opens up the other case and takes out his business card. "Here is my personal number," he hands his card to Rick.

"Okay, Bill, we will prove that the Aliens and UFOs are here. I have seen them first hand!" he says with a convincing look.

Bill closes both briefcases and stands. "Well, we will get to the bottom of this soon."

Rick stands, also, "it sounds like a plan. They are good; I hope we can pull it off."

Bill picks up his briefcases and heads to the door and opens it. "I'll be talking to you soon." He walks out as he closes the door.

Rick stands there as Bill leaves, thinking. *I hope that he can pull this one off. I'll give it my best tomorrow; I'll make sure that Jordan pays for everything.*

It's the following day after they left the ship. Jordan is thinking about everything that happened on the ship with Brayden. He is lying in bed wondering how long it's going to take for Brayden to call wanting to talk about everything. He didn't have to think long, as Brayden comes walking into his bedroom.

"Get out of bed, sleepy head," Brayden says, as he pulls the chair over from Jordan's desk and takes a seat.

Jordan lays there looking at Brayden. "It's only eight o'clock in the morning," he says, as he looks at his clock.

Brayden, sitting there with a big grin, "yep, it's eight."

Jordan sits up in bed, "you didn't sleep much last night, did you?"

"Nope, not much. I had too much to think about. You really pulled one on me and this is how I'm going to pay you back." Brayden smiles at Jordan. "Now you have to answer all my questions."

Jordan sits there thinking, *just what I thought would happen; I'm in for it today.* "Did you have breakfast?" he asks.

"No, I didn't," Brayden replies.

Jordan moves around and sits on the edge of the bed. "Call the trolley; I'm going to take you out for breakfast at the Idle Hour in Spring Lake."

Brayden takes his phone out of his pocket. "We haven't been there in a while; I really like that place." He makes the call. "Twenty minutes," he says as Jordan is up and getting ready.

Jordan, looking at Brayden, "I know that you want to talk, let's hold off until after breakfast. Then we will have a nice walk to our place in the dunes overlooking the lake."

Brayden gets up and puts the chair back by Jordan's desk. "I can do that. I'm now just thinking about which good breakfast that I'm going to choose off their menu."

Jordan stands there looking at Brayden, "you remember the Idle Hour's menu?"

Brayden walks to the bedroom door, "who can forget? Let's go sit on the front porch and wait for the trolley."

Jordan follows Brayden to the kitchen where Jordan's mother is sitting with the newspaper and a cup of coffee.

"Good morning. Brayden and I are going out to breakfast," Jordan says as they are leaving.

Mother looks up, "what's the occasion?"

Brayden stops and turns to Jordan's mother. "We are celebrating my surprise," he says with a smile.

"Jordan told me all about it, congratulations," she replies as she takes a sip of her coffee.

"Thanks," replies Brayden as he opens the door to leave.

"See you later," says Jordan as he follows Brayden.

They walk around to the front porch and take their seats looking out at the road.

"I want to know more about the learning sessions that I'm going to have," says Brayden, as he is looking out at the road.

Jordan looks at Brayden, "I can understand what you are thinking. Your sessions will be slightly different from mine. It will take a little explaining; let's discuss this later."

Brayden turns to Jordan, "okay, later. But for now, I'm getting hungry." He looks out at the road, "here comes the trolley."

They get up and head to the driveway as the trolley pulls in and stops. They get in and off they go to the Idle Hour in Spring Lake.

After a good breakfast, they call the trolley to pick them up and take them back to Jordan's home.

As they get off of the trolley, Brayden turns to Jordan. "Now I can't wait to get to our spot on the dunes so we can talk."

Jordan smiles, "yes, Brayden, let's go." Jordan knows that he will be pumped with questions all the way there.

They walk by the house door and Jordan opens it and sticks his head in. "We are back and heading up to the campsite," he yells to his mother.

She yells back, "okay."

Jordan closes the door and they go on their way up towards the campsite area.

As they are walking the questions start like Jordan thought they would.

"How long have you known that the new transmitters were approved?" Brayden asks.

Jordan keeps walking, "not long, only a few days."

"So, you planned everything in just a couple days?"

Jordan grins, thinking about a good comeback to Brayden's question. "It didn't take me long; I have been through all the learning sessions. I'm smart."

Brayden pats Jordan on the back, "yeah, I have seen you in action," remembering the Rick incident in the sporting goods store. "I'm going to be smart like you soon."

They keep walking up the path. "Yes, you will. But it will be a different type of smart," replies Jordan.

Brayden stops, "what do you mean by that?" he asks.

Jordan keeps walking, "come on, Brayden. We can stop and talk when we get to the beach."

Brayden catches up with Jordan, "okay, I just need to know about the learning sessions."

"Yes, I know, Brayden, I know," Jordan replies, as he has been listening to Brayden's thoughts all morning. He has had his transmitter tuned into Brayden so he could be forewarned of all the questions that are going through Brayden's head.

Questions

They reach their nice spot on the top of the dunes overlooking Lake Michigan. It's always a good place to enjoy the view and relax.

They both take their seats in the beach sand and look out at the lake. "This is always nice," says Jordan as he runs his hands through the warm sand.

Brayden looks at Jordan, "okay, we are here. Now you can explain the difference between your learning sessions and the ones that I'm going to have."

Jordan had turned off his transmitter from listening to Brayden's thoughts a little while ago. He knows that Brayden is ready to start shooting questions his way.

Jordan looks down at the beach, "your learning sessions will be like mine; but different in what you will learn." He looks out at the lake, thinking of a way to explain the difference. "Okay, technology will be your base of your learning sessions."

Brayden gives Jordan a questioning look, "technology?"

Jordan looks at Brayden, smiling, "yes, technology. You have been chosen by the Elder's, how do I put it?" he looks back out at the lake. "Okay," he turns back and looks at Brayden. "You are going to be the next Albert Einstein."

Brayden starts to laugh, "me? Einstein? Yeah, right!"

Jordan had talked with Tarke before they left the ship and Tarke had told him what the Elders' plan is for

Brayden. That had set Jordan back thinking about how Brayden would handle his new knowledge. What will Brayden's mind come up with for life here on earth?

"Yes, Brayden, you are going to be given more knowledge than people here on earth can even begin to think of." Jordan is still looking at Brayden, "this isn't anything to laugh about, Brayden. This is serious; you have to take this seriously."

Brayden looks out at the lake, now thinking about what Jordan just told him. "I'm going to be the next Albert Einstein," he pauses for a minute. "Me, wow, is this how Albert Einstein got his smarts?"

"I asked Tarke the same question. He just smiled and didn't answer," Jordan answers.

They both just sit there thinking about everything that has been happening to them this summer.

Brayden grins as he looks at Jordan. "I know what has happened to you and me this summer is true. But, wow, it's almost too much to believe."

"I was just thinking about the same thing." Jordan lays back in the sand and looks up at the blue sky. "I'm from somewhere out there."

Brayden's since of humor comes out, "and don't let Rick know that."

Jordan chuckles as he is laying there. "Maybe I should let him know."

Brayden looks at Jordan, "that's enough talk about icky Ricky." Brayden turns and looks back out at the water, "didn't they teach you all of the technical stuff, too?"

Jordan sits up, "yes, they did, but in a different way. I know about the use of the technology. You will be taught about the technology and how it works." He turns to Brayden, "it's like this, I have a radio and know how to use it. You will be taught how to make the radio and how it works."

"Okay, I see how your Einstein example fits," Brayden answers. "So, I'm going to know what makes your Explorer work and fly."

"Eventually, I'm sure you will," Jordan answers.

Brayden gives Jordan a worried look, "I'm scared. I don't know if I can handle it."

Jordan reaches over and gives Brayden a pat on the back. "You will handle it just fine," Jordan smiles as he looks at the lake. "I predict that you are going to have a lot of fun with your new knowledge."

Brayden gives Jordan a small grin. "You may be right." He looks up at the sky and smiles, "Brayden Einstein."

Jordan chuckles, "you just might become famous." He looks at Brayden, "news flash; Brayden Hudson has miraculously designed the first kiteboard that doesn't need a kite to glide across the water."

They both start laughing as the futuristic stories start and they lay back in the warm sand and dream.

Bill's plan

Bill gives Rick a call, "hi, Rick, do you have the coordinates yet?"

"Darn, no, I don't. I have been busy with work So I will be able to get another car," he answers. I'll get your coordinates today."

Bill responds, "okay. Can we get together tomorrow?"

"Yes, how about around four in the afternoon? I had to get a new job and I have to work until three," Rick answers, hoping to get together with Bill and get the plan on the move.

"Okay, I'll see you at four tomorrow," Bill replies and hangs up the phone.

Rick puts his phone down and fetches his GPS. After checking the batteries and giving it a try, he calls a cab. A little while later Rick hears a car horn. He grabs his GPS and hurries out the door to the cab.

He gets in the cab and gives him a location where he wants to go. The driver asks, "you have a home that you want to go to?"

Rick answers, "no, I just want to take a walk along the lake and I know a nice place to start."

"Okay, just tell me when to stop and let you off," the driver answers as he drives to Rick's described location.

About fifteen minutes later the cab driver asks, "are we getting close?"

Rick is trying to be extra nice because he will need a ride back home in an hour or so. "You are getting close; just another mile."

The driver proceeds for a mile, "how is this?" he asks.

It is close enough for Rick, "yep, this will do."

The cab driver pulls over to the side of the road. "That will be $7.50, sir."

Rick, thinking about Bill's and his plan, is happy to pay the price for his ride. He pulls out his wallet, "here is ten dollars. Be back here in two hours and I'll have another ten for you to take me back home."

The driver smiles, "Okay, it's eleven, I'll be back here at one o'clock."

Rick closes the cab door and heads into the wooded area thinking, *it's worth paying that jerk twenty bucks just to get here. I'll get it back in the end.* Rick turns on his GPS and marks the spot where he is to give Bill a starting point. Then he starts walking towards Jordan's camping area. He is thinking about the plan and how the Alien's had got him. He stops and thinks out a plan on how he is going to get the camp coordinates without being obvious. He looks at his GPS and remembers the mark button thinking. *That's easy I'll keep the GPS in my pocket and just walk through the camp and press the mark button. This will be easy.* He gets close to the camp and puts the GPS in his pocket and keeps his finger on the mark button as he quickly walks through Jordan's camping area. Half of the way through, he presses the button and then takes his hand out of his pocket, leaving the GPS there. He wants to be safe, so he continues another two hundred yards before he stops and takes a look at the GPS. "Got it," he says out loud with a grin. He puts the GPS back into his pocket and turns around to head back to the starting point where the cab dropped him off. Just in case he marks the coordinates again as he quickly walks back through Jordan's campsite.

Rick reaches the starting point where the cab will pick him up and looks at his watch. Dang it, I was too fast; I did this in only an hour. He calls the cab company and gives them directions to where he is, then sits down by a tree and waits for his ride home. Twenty minutes go by and Rick is starting to get upset. He stands up to look down the road. No cab, he mumbles in disgust and sits back down. Another twenty minutes and he can see a cab coming. He stands up and waves his hand so the driver would know it was him that called.

The cab comes to a stop in front of him, and Rick opens the door and gets in. "What's your problem?" he says in an angry voice.

The cab driver looks back at Rick, "I was on another run when I received the call to pick you up."

Rick slams the cab door shut, "it's been almost an hour waiting for the darn cab company to send me a stupid driver."

The cab driver picks up his radio mic and turns around. "I can cancel this run if you continue with your attitude."

Rick looks at the driver, "take me home." He sits back and looks out of the window.

"Give me your address please, " the driver asks nicely.

Rick spits out his address and continues looking out the window.

The cab driver rolls his eyes back, then turns the cab around and takes Rick home.

It's four o'clock exactly when Rick hears a knock on his door. He is expecting Bill when he opens the door to see him standing there.

"Good afternoon, Rick,"

"Hi. Bill. I have your coordinates," Rick replies with a smile.

Bill still standing at the door, "are you going to let me in?" he says with a grin on his face.

"Sure, come in. I want to hear your plans," Rick says as he steps aside to let Bill in.

They walk over to the table and take their seats. Bill opens his briefcase and takes out his papers and a pen. "Okay, give me the coordinates," Bill says, as he is ready to write them down.

Rick gets up and walks over to his table by the couch and gets his GPS. He heads back to the table as he turns his GPS on. He sits down and reads the coordinates for Bill.

"It was easy getting the coordinates; it's just the stupid cab company getting me back home. I can't wait to be able to get another car."

"Yes, I bet it is hard without wheels," answers Bill.

"Yeah, those Aliens wrecked my car, and all I got out of it was two hundred dollars for scrap."

Bill looks up at Rick after making sure the coordinates were written down right. "Well, there isn't much that we can do about it. How do you sue Aliens?" he says, not wanting to show any emotion.

"Okay, Rick, here is how the plan will work," Bill looking at his paperwork. "We figure that they are watching you and me." Bill looks at Rick, "you got the coordinates discreetly, I hope?"

Rick smiling, "I had my GPS in my pocket and marked the coordinates hidden that way. I just walked straight through Jordan's campsite without stopping."

"Sounds good." Bill looks back at his papers, "like I said, we believe that they are watching us. So, we will pay your friend, Jordan, a visit as Tom my associate will be up at Jordan's campsite placing five micro cameras." Bill looks up and grins, "they will be paying attention to us and not the campsite. The micro cameras have a five-day battery life and four hours of video and sound recording time. If anything happens within the five days, we will have high-quality video and sound of it." Bill smiles, "Tom is a very good geocacher and is used to hiding and finding small items. He is at the top of our list to use the coordinates and do the hiding."

Rick is smiling, knowing exactly what Bill is telling him. "Geocaching is why I purchased my GPS. I know what you are telling me. I have tried to find some of those darn small geocache hides."

Bill closes his briefcase, "that's the plan. I'll talk it over with my colleagues and then get back to you with a time."

They both get up and Bill walks over to the door. "I'll give you a call as soon as possible."

"Everything sounds good; I can't wait to get those Aliens," Rick says, as he opens the door for Bill.

Bill leaves and Rick walks over to his couch, sits down and puts his feet up on the coffee table.

Another get-together

Jordan finishes his breakfast with his mother, and she says, "You and Brayden don't have too many nice days for camping. Brayden will be going back to school next month."

Jordan finishes his glass of milk, "yes, you'er right. It feels different to me because I don't have to go back to school this year."

Mother smiles, "my little boy has graduated. Now look what you are looking at in your future."

"Yes, it's been quite an adventure so far this summer." He smiles as he looks at his mother. "You know what I mean; it's nice to be able to talk to you about it."

Jordan still doesn't really come out too much in detail about the ship and the Aliens.

"I think I'm going to give Brayden a call," he says as he takes care of his dishes.

"I'll tell you what... I will make up some homemade peanut butter cookies. Brayden always talks about Grandmother's cookies; I'll give him my cookies to talk about."

"Sounds good; I'll let you surprise him." Jordan walks to his room to get his phone so he can give Brayden a call.

He sits on his bed and calls Brayden, "hey, do you have any plans today?"

"Nope, I was just going to give you a call," answers Brayden. "I will hop on my bike and be over in a short. Then we can figure something out."

"Sounds good, I'll see you in a little while." They both hang up their phones.

Jordan walks back to the kitchen, "Brayden is riding his bike over in a little while," he tells mother.

"I'm glad you told me, he will smell the cookies when he comes in the door," she says with a smile.

Jordan, looking at his mother, "I'm going to the porch and wait for him."

"I'll have the cookies ready in about an hour." Mother turns back to the counter and resumes mixing the cookie batter.

Jordan walks out on the front porch and takes a seat. He leans back to enjoy the slight breeze in what is turning out to be a nice sunny day.

Jordan sat there enjoying the weather as he is thinking about something that he and Brayden could do. He looks down the road and can see Brayden coming on his bike. Jordan stands and walks to the driveway to meet Brayden, thinking *we need to go to the side door so Brayden can smell Mom's cookies.*

Brayden rides into the driveway and up to Jordan. "I get an official greeting by Captain Jordan," he says with a smile.

Jordan grins, "park your bike over there, Mate," Jordan says as he points to the garage.

Brayden parks his bike and walks back to Jordan. He looks at the house, "I smell peanut butter cookies."

Jordan, looking at Brayden, "Brayden, Mother wants to surprise you with her cookies."

Brayden lowers his voice as he looks at Jordan, "okay, I got it."

Jordan grins and they walk to the house and the door, Brayden following Jordan as they enter. Brayden looks at Jordan's mother, "yum, I smell cookies baking."

Mother smiles, "I'm making some special cookies for you."

"I can't wait to try them," he says not wanting to tell her that he knows what kind of cookies that they are.

"When they are done, I'll let you know," she answers.

"Thanks, Mom," says Jordan as they head to his room.

They enter Jordan's bedroom and Jordan sits on the edge of his bed. Brayden pulls over the desk chair and takes his seat. "I have been thinking, why don't we invite Pete for another campout? I had a lot of fun with him."

Jordan thinks for a minute, "I think that I can get that approved."

Jordan's mother walks into the room, not looking happy. "Jordan, you have a couple people at the front door. I don't think that you are going to be happy to meet with them."

Jordan stands, "who are they?"

Mother replies, "that guy that gave us a hard time up at the campsite. And the other fella is that investigator man."

Jordan looks at his mother, "Mom, tell them that I will be there in a couple minutes."

She nods her head and walks out of the room.

Jordan turns to Brayden, "this is going to be fun." Brayden smiles, "you are going to let me have fun with them, aren't you?"

"Yes, have at them and I'll follow your lead; let's go." They both head to the front door.

Jordan stops before he opens the door and looks at Brayden, "be nice." Then he opens the door and they walk out on the porch to see Rick and Bill sitting there waiting for him.

Jordan looks at them, "Hi, Rick, what brings you two here?"

Bill looks at Jordan, "Rick has been telling me about you and a connection with Aliens."

Brayden smiles then he turns and walks back into the house.

Jordan thinks Brayden a message, *where are you going?*

Brayden messages his reply, *I'll be right back.*

Jordan doesn't switch to listen to Brayden's thoughts. He knows that whatever he is up to will be good.

Rick, looking at Jordan, "you can't deny it, Jordan; I saw it and you know that I did."

Jordan, trying to eat up some time, walks over and picks up another chair and brings it by them. He sits down and looks at Bill, "so, apparently, you have been talking with Rick about possible sightings."

"Yes, I have been interviewing Rick about his report that he filed with us."

Jordan receives a message from Brayden, *look out, the Aliens are coming.* The front door opens and Brayden comes walking out wearing Jordan's Alien green wetsuit.

He looks directly at Rick, "I come in peace, earthling."

Rick gives Brayden an angry look, "knock it off you idiot goofball."

Bill steps in quickly, trying to keep their conversation civil, "nice outfit, what is your name?"

Brayden looks at Bill with a straight face, "I'm Vader; I come from the planet Goton."

Bill replies, "hi, Vader; welcome to our world," he says trying to play around with Brayden. He turns to Jordan, "so about Rick's report. He states that he came upon you one day and saw a UFO land in front of you."

Brayden looks at Jordan, "was that the day when Rick was drunk?" he asks; because if Rick tries to do something, Jordan can freeze him in his place.

Rick stands up quickly, "you, ..."

Bill quickly puts his hand on Rick's arm, "Rick, calm down."

Jordan calmly stands, "I think that it's time for you guys to leave."

Brayden, looking at Rick and Bill and can't help himself, "I'm done playing with you. You don't know who you are messing with." He thinks about what he just said, so he grabs the chair that Jordan was sitting in and picks it up, trying to look bad.

Bill looks at Rick, still holding his arm, "let's go." They start walking to Bill's car. "Rick turns and looks at Jordan and Brayden, "one of these days," and he gets into Bill's car and they back out of the driveway.

Jordan looks at Brayden, "what was that? You really got on Rick personally, saying that he was drunk."

Brayden sits down with a big grin, "I know that it wasn't nice. I felt safe with you there so I thought that I would discredit Rick's word."

Jordan, thinking about what Brayden just told him, "yes, I guess you did. That should give Bill something to think about." Jordan gets up out of his seat, "I bet you the cookies are ready. By the way," he looks at Brayden, "they don't know who they are dealing with."

They go into the house to see Jordan's mother and have some cookies.

Get together with Pete

After talking with Brayden, a camping weekend was planned. After yesterday, Jordan figures that it is time to go to the ship. During his time on the ship, he can talk to Tarke about getting time off for Pete. It's been a few days now since he has been on the job and up to date with everything.

After breakfast, Jordan walks into the living room to see his mother. "Mom, I'm going to spend the day on the ship." He sits down for a few minutes. "Brayden and I have made plans to camp out this weekend. I'm going to see if Pete can get the weekend off and camp with us."

Mother replies, "in your new position on the space ship, you should be there." She puts her book down, "I like Pete; he is a good man." She turns to Jordan with a smile, "and now knowing that Pete is your brother, you two should be able to get together."

Jordan gets up and walks over and gives his mother a big hug. "Thanks for being so understanding. I love you."

"I love you too, Jordy," she says after her unexpected hug.

Jordan, standing there looking at Mother, "it's time for me to go. I'll see you and Dad later this evening."

"Have a good day," she replies, as Jordan heads out to go up to the camping area.

Jordan heads out of the house and starts walking up the path to the campsite where he will have his Explorer waiting. As he is walking to the campsite, he is thinking about the last time that he had talked to Tarke about his Rick problems. *Tarke told me to believe in my powers and decisions. I do believe.* He keeps walking, *Brayden was right yesterday. Rick and Bill don't know who they are dealing with.* He stops for a moment, thinking, *Rick has brought Bill into the equation and how many more? All I know is that being subtle isn't going to work.* Jordan looks around, having made up his mind; then resumes his walk to the campsite. When he reaches the camping area, he looks around for a couple minutes. He stands there looking at the fire pit thinking. *It's okay; nothing is going to happen today. Then he commands the Explorer to come into view.* The Explorer comes into view and Jordan gets in and pulls the slider down to invisible, then leaves.

He cruises over Lake Michigan for a few minutes enjoying the view then drops into the water towards the main ship. Upon docking, he exits the Explorer and walks through the bridge into the ship. One of the crew members is walking by. "Hello, Jordan. Welcome back," he says as he passes by.

Jordan's transceiver is telling him that Tarke is on the lower level. Jordan messages Tarke, *hi, Tarke. I'm on the ship. I'm going to have a talk with Harec; then I'll catch up with you.*

Tarke replies, *good. I'll be in my office for a little while.*

Good; I'll see you in a bit, Jordan replies.

Jordan walks around to the med room to catch up with Harec. His transceiver had let him know that is where Harec is located. Jordan walks in the door to see Harec sitting at his desk hard at work.

Harec hears Jordan come in and turns around. "Hi, Jordan, what can I do for you today?" he asks.

He walks up beside Harec, "I have a problem that I need to discuss with you."

Harec looks at Jordan, "have a seat. Tell me how I can help you."

Jordan takes a seat, "I still have the Rick problem."

Harec grins, "still, after Karen used the disabler a bit harshly on his electronics?"

"Yes, that did upset him. Now he has a vendetta against me." Jordan sits back. "He is now bringing others into his quest to expose us." He looks at Harec, "as you know, he did see the Explorer and Pete."

Jordan receives a message from Tarke, *I'm on my way back to my office.*

Jordan replies, *thanks for letting me know. I'm having a discussion with Harec. I'll catch up with you in a little while.*

No problem, take your time, Tarke messages.

Jordan continues his conversation with Harec for another twenty minutes before heading to meet with Tarke.

Jordan walks into Tarke's office and takes a seat at Tarke's desk.

Tarke looks up from his monitor, "you had a good talk with Harec."

Jordan grins, "I sure did, as you probably know."

"Yes, I did listen in. I will say this, I agree," Tarke answers and smiles; "yes, Pete can have the weekend off."

Jordan smiles, "you sneaky guy; I'm going to start listening to your thoughts."

Tarke gives Jordan a smiling wink, "you're, learning. That is what I was thinking."

"I hadn't thought of that; I guess that I would be intruding on your thoughts," Jordan replies.

Tarke looks Jordan in the eyes with a straight face, "consider it part of your learning skills. I want you to know what I'm doing and thinking." He smiles, "there are no secrets between us."

Jordan stands and holds his hand out to shake Tarke's hand. "I agree, thank you for your trust."

Tarke stands to shake Jordan's hand, "friends forever."

Tarke sits back down, "so another camping trip for Pete."

Tarke smiles. Then Jordan smiles. "I like that idea, your first. I'll go to the leisure room and wait there." Jordan walks out with a grin.

"I'll see you in a few minutes." Then he calls Pete to his office.

Jordan walks into the leisure room and joins in on a conversation with a few crew members.

Pete walks into Tarke's office, "sir, you called me."

"Yes, I did. I have some important business for you Saturday and Sunday. It is my command that you keep those two days completely open," says Tarke with a serious look.

"Yes, sir. Saturday and Sunday are yours," Pete replies wondering what is going on.

"Okay, that's it for now," Tarke says, as he looks back at his monitor.

Pete, a bit baffled, walks out of the office. Tarke grins and messages Jordan, *it's your turn.*

Jordan receives the message; then messages Pete. *Pete, I'm in the leisure room. If you have a few minutes, stop in. I have a question for you.*

Pete was just walking by the leisure room, so he steps in to see Jordan. "Hi, Brother; what's up?"

Jordan says, "let's go over to the table if you have time. I have something really good to ask you."

Pete smiles as he is taking a seat. "What's up?" he asks wondering Jordan has to ask him.

"Brayden and I have been talking about the last time that you camped with us. We actually had a great time even though there was an interruption." Jordan smiles knowing what is going on, "any way, we are going to camp out this weekend and we want you to join us."

Pete looks at Jordan for a moment with a sad look, "I can't. Tarke just instructed me to keep Saturday and Sunday open. I don't know what his plans are, but I have my instructions."

Jordan looks at Pete and starts to smile as Tarke puts his hand on Pete's shoulder. Pete looks back to see Tarke, "you guys!" Looking at Tarke, "is camping with my brother why I was to keep Saturday and Sunday clear?"

They start laughing; the other crew members in the room knew what was going to happen. Jordan had told them earlier.

Tarke looks around the room thinking that it is good to have a little fun with them. "I have to go back to work; I'll talk to you later, Jordan."

Pete is smiling now, "I'll be at your house early Saturday morning."

Jordan, looking at Pete, "it's a plan." He stands up. But now I have business to discuss with Tarke.

Pete gets up and walks out to the room with Jordan.

Pete arrives

It's early Saturday morning, and Jordan's father is going into the garage as Pete comes walking up.

"Good morning, Mr. Kingston," he says.

Jordan's father turns to see Pete, "good morning. You are here early today."

Pete smiles, "I couldn't sleep last night. I kept thinking about camping this weekend with Jordan and Brayden."

"Jordan is still in bed. Go on inside; Gloria is in the kitchen. I have to head out to work," Jordan's father says as he opens the garage door.

"Have a good day," says Pete, as Jordan's father gets into the car.

Pete walks to the house door and opens it, "hello," he says before he walks in.

Mother can see the door and Pete, "come on in, Pete."

Pete comes in and walks over to the table where Jordan's mother is reading the paper. "How are you doing, Mrs. Kingston?"

She smiles, "I'm doing great. How about you?"

"Great, also. I have been looking forward to camping out with Jordan and Brayden all night," Pete answers.

"That's what brings you here so early in the day," she replies.

Pete puts his hand on a chair, "may I," he asks.

Mother looks at Pete, "yes, please do." She looks over at the kitchen counter, "help yourself to a cup of coffee. The cups are in the cupboard above the coffee maker."

Pete gets a cup of coffee and sits down with Jordan's mother. She puts the newspaper down, "did Jordan tell you that he had company the other day?"

Pete gives her a questioning look, "no, I haven't been able to talk with him much lately."

She takes a sip of her coffee, "he had that Rick fellow, and some investigator man stop by. I'm sure Jordan will love to tell you about it." Jordan's mother looks over to the hallway, "good morning," she says, as Jordan walks into the kitchen.

Jordan looks surprised as he sits down at the table. "it's not even eight in the morning; what brings you here so early?"

Pete grins, "I'm ready for camping. I got the camp set up and ready while you were all snuggled up in bed."

Jordan looks at Pete, "okay, that was good. You might get away with that with Brayden, but not with me." Jordan smiles, "but it was good."

Pete looking at Jordan, "I forgot, Tarke has been teaching you well."

"Did you have breakfast?" Jordan asks.

Pete looks at his cup of coffee, "this is it."

Jordan gets up and goes over to the cupboard and gets out a box of Raisin Bran cereal and a couple bowls. He puts a bowl in front of Pete; then gets the milk and a couple spoons. "Here you go, breakfast," he says with a smile.

They both eat their breakfast; then head out to get the camp set up. They decide to bring everything up to the campsite the old fashion way, using Jordan's father's tractor and trailer. They load everything up and Jordan lets Pete drive the tractor.

Pete looks at Jordan as he sits on the tractor, "I know how to drive this, but it is a first time for me."

Twenty minutes later they have the trailer unloaded.

Jordan looks at Pete, "let's take a break and go over to our sitting log."

Pete agrees and they go over to take their seats.

Pete looks at Jordan, "your mother told me that you had a couple visitors the other day."

Jordan smiles as he turns to Pete, "I sure did. That is what I want to talk to you about."

Pete looks out at all of the camping equipment sitting there. "That can wait; tell me about your visit."

Jordan, still looking at Pete, "it's a long story, but I'll make it short for you. Brayden won't be here until around noon, so we have time to take care of a few things." He looks at the camping equipment, "Rick and his UFO investigator friend stopped by, supposedly to ask me a few questions. What they don't know is that I tuned into their thoughts." He turns to Pete, "their visit was just a distraction. While they were trying to get something out of me; there was another fellow up here hiding small cameras."

"And they are here now?" Pete asks.

Jordan looks around, "they sure are. You and I have both landed here; so that, in Rick's eyes, would be a payday."

"So, our first job today is to disable them," Jordan says, as he stands and walks over to a box that they carried up to the campsite. Jordan opens the box and takes out two small items.

Pete looks at the two gadgets that Jordan has in his hands. "I recognize those, an electronics detector and the disabler."

Jordan looks at Pete, "Harec set me up with these. Let's go on a hunt, we have five small cameras to find."

Jordan puts the disabler in his pocket then turns on the electronics detector. "Wow, this thing is going nuts. It's showing me all five cameras."

"Go for the closest one," Pete says, as he looks at the detectors screen.

The detector takes them to the closest one. Jordan looks at Pete, "this guy hid this mini camera pretty well."

Pete answers, "he sure did. He can't hide it from the detector, though. Let's leave it here and mark its location."

Jordan looks around, "that sounds like a good idea. It will be fun to see how they are placed."

Pete looks around and finds a long stick and puts it in the ground next to the camera. "Next," he says and they head to the next one. They do the same for the next camera. They proceeded to find the third camera and Jordan stops and looks up, "look at that." He points up high in a tree, "it's way up there." He points at the small camera hidden high up on a tree limb, "that guy is good."

Pete marks that camera location and then they find the last two cameras. With all five locations marked they walk back to the fire pit area.

Jordan looks around, "he had this area covered well."

"He sure does," Pete agrees as he looks around. "What are your plans with these?"

"Now that I see the creativity and dedication that went into hiding these, I have to think about it," Jordan answers, as he walks over and grabs a couple camp chairs. He brings the chairs over to the fire pit area and hands one to Pete. "I don't want to make a quick decision; let's talk about it," and he sits down in his camping chair.

Pete sits in his chair, "what was your original plan?"

"I was going to find them and then use the disabler on them. Fry them, as Brayden would say," answers Jordan.

Pete looks at Jordan, "that's your answer." He smiles, "ask Brayden. He is clever enough to come up with a creative solution."

Jordan smiles, "oh, what the heck. I'll put it to Brayden when he arrives." He looks back to all the camping gear lying there, "let's clear our minds about the cameras and set up camp."

Pete stands, "that sounds like a good idea." they both get busy getting everything together and in place. In no time at all the camp is set up.

Jordan looks at Pete, "you can drive the tractor down and I'll ride in the trailer." Pete hops on the tractor. With Jordan relaxing in the trailer, they head back down to the house.

Brayden arrives

Jordan and Pete are sitting on the front porch listening to the radio. They are talking, as Brayden rides in the driveway on his bike.

Pete spots Brayden first, "here comes Brayden."

Jordan stands to greet Brayden, "Hi, Brayden. Park your bike; we'll be here waiting for you."

Brayden rides to the garage and parks his bike inside. A couple minutes later, here comes Brayden up on the porch. "Hi, guys, are we ready for camping tonight?"

"We sure are; we have been waiting for you all morning," Pete says as he is waiting for a smart reply.

Brayden looks at Pete, "I would have come earlier, but we would have had to wake up Jordan."

Pete smiles with Brayden's reply, "I woke him up at seven thirty this morning."

Jordan looks at Brayden, "he sure did, and we have the camp set up."

Brayden smiles, "good, then I don't have to do anything but enjoy. What are we doing here?"

Jordan looks at Pete, "let's go."

Pete stands up, "come on, Brayden. We have a question for you when we get up to the camp."

"You can't ask your question now?" Brayden asks.

Jordan turns, "let's go. I would rather show you some things around the campsite, then ask our question."

Brayden answers, "Oh, okay." And they head around to the backyard, then up the path. They get a little way up to the camp, and the question is bugging him. "Come on, can't you tell me something?"

They keep walking the path and Jordan replies, "remember when Rick and Bill stopped over the other day?"

"My Vader day; yes, I do remember." Brayden answers.

"I tuned into their thoughts. They were here just to take the attention away from a guy that was up in our camping area. He was cleverly hiding five micro cameras," explains Jordan.

Brayden stops, "five cameras?"

Jordan turns to Brayden, "come on, let's get up to the camp."

Brayden catches up with Jordan, "why didn't you tell me before today?"

Jordan looks over to Brayden, "I had to think about it, and I didn't want to ruin the day."

Pete jumps into the conversation, "it's under control. We left the cameras for you to see."

Brayden replies, "Thanks, I can't wait to see them."

They enter the camping area and Brayden looks around. "Nice, you guys have everything setup."

Pete answers, "I told you that it was set up."

Brayden walks over by the fire pit. "I see that you guys have your camp chairs set up. Where is mine?"

Pete smiles, "what, we have to do everything? Get your own chair."

212

Brayden looks at Pete with a straight face; then turns to get his camping chair with a big smile. He comes back with his chair and sets it up. "Now, show me those cameras."

Jordan and Pete walk around the campsite area showing Brayden all the cameras. Then they head back to their chairs and sit down to talk.

Brayden looks over at Jordan, "they are getting clever. The cameras are painted well, the same color as the trees. And whoever that guy is, he hid them well."

"Yes, he did. I used an electronics detector that I got from Harec to help me find them, "replies Jordan.

"Cool. So when you found each one of them, you fried them?" asks Brayden.

Jordan pulls the disabler out of his pocket and looks at it. "You know, I sure wanted to. But, no, they are recording right now," he says as he looks around. "Pete and I decided to leave them alone for now."

Brayden looks at Pete, then Jordan, "why?"

Jordan looks over at Pete, "like your first thought, Brayden, you want to fry them. Think about it. What happened after Karen fried Rick's game cameras?" He looks at Brayden, "look at what we have now. We have Bill to deal with and now five cameras."

"I guess you are right. Now, what can we do?" Brayden asks.

Pete smiles, "that is why we have waited for you." Pete looks at Jordan, "I'll ask him." Jordan nods his head in a yes motion. "Our question… we need to do something other than fry those cameras. You are creative; we need your ideas."

Jordan, looking at Brayden, "come on, <u>B</u>uddy, let's put a stop to them." Jordan smiles, "I know that I have had all those learning sessions. But with your head and mine together we can do it."

Brayden smiles with Jordan's response, "okay, let's think about it. For now, let's turn those darn cameras off."

Pete looks at Jordan, "I agree, I'll turn them off."

Jordan agrees, "Yes, turn them off."

Pete and Brayden go to each one of the cameras and turn them off. Jordan stays in his seat watching them as he tries to come up with a plan.

They come back talking as they take their seats.

Brayden looks at Jordan, Pete and I were talking and think that we should erase the memory cards in each of the cameras."

"There is most likely a lot of incriminating video on those cameras," Pete adds.

Jordan replies, "good idea. Let's get the cards and I'll transport them to Harec to permanently delete anything that is on them."

All three of them get up and remove the memory cards from the cameras. Jordan takes them back to the camp table and sets them down.

Brayden looks at the cards then turns to Jordan. "This is like when Harec transported the transfers to the conference room for us. You know how to do that, too?"

"Yes, I do, there are a lot of things that I can do that you don't know. They were in my learning sessions." Jordan smiles as he messages Harec, *Harec I have five memory cards that I'm going to transport to you. I need you to permanently erase their memories.* Harec replies, *send them to me, I'll get right on them. Do you want copies of what is on them?* Jordan messages back, *sure you can make copies for me.* Harec messages back, *okay I'll make copies and transport them back to where you sent them from.* Jordan transports them to Harec.

Brayden stands there, knowing that Jordan is messaging Harec. Jordan turns to Brayden, "watch." He turns to look at the memory cards and they fade away.

Brayden looks up to Jordan with a grin, "that's just too cool."

Brayden and Jordan walk back to the fire pit where Pete is sitting.

Brayden sits there looking out into the woods, thinking. Then all of a sudden he turns to Jordan. "I have a plan." He stands up in front of Jordan and Pete. It's a long plan." He looks at Jordan. "I hope that you can pull this off."

Brayden goes through his plan step by step with Jordan and Pete. They watch Brayden go through hand gestures and walks around the fire pit explaining the plan. Jordan and Pete are almost in tears from laughter watching Brayden. The best thing is that it made perfect sense. Brayden sits down as Jordan and Pete gain their composure.

Jordan looks at Brayden, "we knew that you would come up with an idea. You did in spades! It's a go as far as I'm concerned.

The plan

Brayden gets out of his camping chair, "okay, I'm going to run home and get my stuff."

Jordan replies, "I'll see you in a while." He looks over at the camp table, "the memory cards are back."

"That didn't take long," Brayden says, as he is walking to the path. "See you later; it won't take me long." Brayden heads down the path.

Pete looks at Jordan, "we got up here earlier and set up everything and now we have to take it down."

Jordan grins, "yes, we do; but it will be worth it."

"You know, this is the second camping trip of mine that Rick has got in the way," says Pete as he folds up the camping chairs.

As Jordan helps Pete with the chairs, he looks over at Pete. "But this time we will put a stop to his shenanigans once and for all."

Pete puts the chairs down on the path, "that's probably true. Brayden did come up with a good idea."

They take the tent down and put everything in a pile on the path. They look at each other when they are done and start to laugh.

"Our camping chairs are in the bottom of the pile," says Jordan.

Pete and Jordan move things around and get the chairs out so they can sit down.

Pete sets up a couple camping chairs as Jordan gets a couple pops out of the cooler. They both sit down and relax with their drinks.

Pete is thinking about the plan as he is looking over at the fire pit. "We need a bunch of cans for later," he tells Jordan.

Jordan smiles, "my dad has been saving cans all summer. Let's go down to the garage and get a few. Maybe we will meet up with Brayden."

Pete leans back in his seat, "teleport them up here," he says with a grin; then takes a sip of his pop.

Jordan smiles, "no, I don't know exactly where they are at. I might teleport the leaf blower up here."

They have fun with their jokes as they finish their drinks. They head down to the garage to get a bag of cans. When they almost get to the back of the house, they see Brayden carrying his sports bag coming their way. They meet up with Brayden, "what are you two coming down here for?" Brayden asks.

"We were thinking that we should come down to the garage and get a bag of my father's cans," Jordan says.

"Good idea, I'll wait here for you," says Brayden, as he sets his sports bag down and takes a seat in the grass.

Pete looks at Jordan, "go ahead and get the cans. I'm going to stay here and visit with Brayden."

"Okay," replies Jordan as he heads to the garage.

Pete sits down alongside of Brayden, "so you have everything that you need?"

Brayden smiles, "I sure do. I can't wait to put it to use."

Pete is thinking, *oh boy, this is going to be good.* He has been around Brayden enough to know that he probably has more in mind than he has told them.

Jordan comes back a little out of breath, "got them."

Pete looking at Jordan, "you didn't have to rush."

"I looked at my watch and we need to step things up. The day is getting short and we have a lot to do," Jordan says, as he gains his breath back.

"I agree," says Brayden as he gets up with his bag.

Jordan looks at Brayden's sports bag, "you have that bag packed."

Brayden just smiles as he heads up the path towards the campsite.

They reach the campsite and Brayden puts his bag down. Looking around he says, "looks good." He looks at Jordan, "do you have the memory cards back in the cameras?"

Pete answers, "yes, we do; all we need to do is turn them on. They have a ten-minute delay when they are turned on. So, if each of us take a couple; we can turn them on and get out of view before they start recording."

Brayden says, "I'll take the one that is up in the tree. You two can take the other four."

"Sounds like a plan," answers Jordan. Jordan is thinking, *It's good, Brayden is taking over with his plan like we agreed that he should.*

They get the cameras started and they get back by all their camping gear.

Talking lightly, they go over the plan with Brayden. With each of them knowing what they are doing, they go into action.

Action....

Pete comes walking into the camping area with his hands full of camping gear. Brayden is alongside him with his hands full, also.

Pete puts his stuff down, "this is hard work."

Brayden answers, "yes, it is. Jordan and I do this all the time. It usually takes us three trips to get everything up here."

Pete looks at everything, "and we have two more trips."

Brayden answers, "yep, if Jordan wasn't helping Grandpa out, it would only be two trips today with his help."

They walk out of the camping area and quietly sit down and take a thirty-minute break.

They do this one more time with another thirty-minute break.

Then on the third time, they come walking into the camping area and set their loads down.

Brayden sets up a camping chair and sits down. "I hope Grandpa is working Jordan hard. We have done everything for him today."

Pete gets a chair also and takes a seat, "but it's fun; I can't complain."

They sit there a few minutes knowing that the cameras are catching everything that they are doing.

After a short rest, they set up the tent and get everything arranged. Pete gets some wood set up in the fire pit and gets a fire started.

Jordan is in his Explorer hovering above Rick's apartment. He puts it in hold mode and gets up from the control area.

He thinks a message to Tarke. *Well, Tarke, I'm here as you probably know. I'm apprehensive but ready to go.*

Tarke replies, *believe, Jordan, believe. You will have no problems. You have the knowledge and the ability.*

Jordan looks out over Grand Haven, *I know I do. Have fun watching; let Brayden's plan begin.*

Jordan teleports down into Rick's living room.

Rick is sitting on his couch when Jordan suddenly appears in front of him. "What the heck," he says, as he jumps up from the couch. "Where the heck did you come from?"

Jordan stands there looking at Rick. "Well, Rick, I thought that it is time that you know who you are dealing with."

Rick answers back quickly, "yeah, Aliens! They got you doing things for them now."

Jordan looks at Rick, "no, Rick, they don't." he turns to the TV and puts his hand out; the TV turns off. Jordan points at the coffee table in front of Rick. The table rises up in the air, as Rick's mouth opens in amazement. "look at me Rick," says Jordan?

Rick looks at Jordan, "you don't want to push me anymore. I have turned off your ability to walk."

Rick, not believing Jordan, tries to move, then looks at Jordan with panic on his face. "I'll get you, one way or another," he says, still being his stubborn belligerent self.

"Okay, Rick, if you want it your way." Jordan puts a freeze on Rick, leaving him not able to move. "Okay, I now can do anything with you that I want. And I'm going to let you see and think about what is happening. If you get too vocal, I'll shut that off, also."

Rick is now frightened; he can't move his arms or legs. He can just look around.

"You want to see a UFO? Mine is right above your house," says Jordan.

Rick looks up at the ceiling, "yeah, right."

"Rick, come on now, be nice." Jordan teleports Rick up into the Explorer, then teleports up.

Rick is standing there in the Explorer as Jordan appears. Jordan puts his hands, on Rick's shoulders and pushes him down into a seat. "There you go, big boy."

I'm going to give you a ride. He sits in the control seat and takes the Explorer out of hold. Up they go, fast. Jordan stops and rotates the Explorer so Rick can see Earth from space. "How do you like your ride?"

Jordan keeps the Explorer on the same angle so Rick can see Earth and heads down fast. He comes down to Muskegon Lake, then over the top of town, out towards

Lake Michigan, then down the shoreline. He slows down to a stop over a wooded area.

Jordan puts the Explorer into hold mode again. He turns to Rick who is now quiet and a bit pale from the ride. "from this point on, I'm going to shut off your ability to speak."

Rick is now shaken with what Jordan is able to do. At this point, he will do anything that Jordan wants. He tries to say something to Jordan but nothing works; he now can only see and hear.

Jordan messages Brayden, *I'm at the edge of the camp with Rick. Are you ready?*

Brayden replies, *yes, come on down.*

Brayden looks at Pete and winks, "I think I hear something out in the woods."

Pete makes a surprise look on his face. "Look it's our friend, Rick," and he gets up to meet with Rick.

Brayden and Pete walk out of the cameras' view. A couple minutes later they come walking back into the cameras' view helping Rick walk. They take him over to Jordan's camping chair and sit him down. They stand there in front of Rick looking at him.

Pete turns to Brayden, "he has been drinking again."

Brayden replies, "he sure has. Look at him; I think that there is something wrong with him. This is happening a lot." Brayden turns to the path, "there's Jordan."

Jordan walks up to them, "oh, no, it's Rick again. He looks like he is drunker than a skunk." Jordan looks at Brayden and Pete, "look what he has on today."

Brayden smiles, "this is how I found him, wandering around in the woods."

Pete looks at Rick, "I think he has gone off the deep end."

"Yes, that is for sure. And when we talk to him, he will say that he doesn't drink. It's too bad Rick, you do need help."

All the time the acting is going on for the cameras, Rick is seeing and listening. He looks around but can't do anything but sit there. He knows what is going on and it is making him mad.

Brayden looks at Jordan and Pete, "well, I guess it's my turn to try to find all his beer cans."

"Yeah, and by the looks of him, you'll find a bunch," replies Pete.

Brayden walks off out of the cameras' view.

Jordan walks over by the tent and grabs the extra camping chair and comes back. He sets up the chair, then puts a couple pieces of wood on the fire. Pete takes a seat as Jordan gets the fire going good.

Jordan sits down and looks at Rick, "boy, Rick, why are you dressed like a girl?"

Rick just sits there not being able to say anything.

"I like that dress; prom night was several months ago. And that hat, that is something else."

Brayden had done some shopping at Goodwill and found a light blue dress. The dress looks like it might have been a bridesmaid's dress. The hat that Rick is wearing is a big red floppy hat that one of the Red Hat ladies would like.

Brayden comes walking back into the cameras' view caring a bag of beer cans. He walks over to Rick and dumps the cans out of the bag in front of Rick. "look at this Rick, I hope that I found them all." Brayden goes over and sits down in his camping chair.

Jordan looks at Brayden, "I guess that I'm going to have to take him home again. We can't have him driving on the road again. He already wrecked one car."

Brayden stands up from his chair, "he's drunk. I brought my Alien costume to have some fun tonight."

"You did; go get it on. We can have some fun with Rick again with it," says Jordan with a smile.

"Okay," says Brayden and he heads into the tent.

Pete looks at Jordan, "do you think Rick is okay? He is just sitting there."

"Yes, he is all right. He is just stone drunk like always," Jordan answers.

They hear a whoop sound and Brayden, fully dressed as an Alien, comes walking towards them. "I'm Vader and I come in peace," he says, as he walks over by Rick. "Hi, earthling; you have a nice hat," he says to Rick. He walks around the camp fire, stopping occasionally, looking back at Rick. He comes around to Pete, "that earthling dresses different than you."

Pete is close to breaking out into laughter as he looks at Brayden. "Yes, Vader, he does dress a bit different."

Brayden walks over to Rick, and looks at him, "you don't smell good either." He shakes his head in his Alien mask and walks off.

Jordan stands, "bye, Vader, safe travels," as Brayden in his Alien costume walks out of the cameras' view.

Pete looks at Jordan, "I'll help you with Rick. It will probably take both of us to get his drunk body down to a cab to take him home."

"Yes, he is hammered again for sure," Jordan answers.

All the time Rick is awake, hearing and watching everything that is going on around him. He is totally frustrated with his situation and not being able to do anything. On one hand, he is mad, but on the other hand, he has become very scared of what they can do. He just wants to go home and stay far away from Jordan and his friends.

Take me home

Brayden comes back and takes his seat by the fire.

Jordan looks at Rick, "I think that it is time to get you home."

That was like hearing music in Rick's ears. He has been wondering when, or if, he would be able to go home.

"I'm ready to get the drunk out of here. I'm tired of looking at him," Pete replies.

They both get up from their seats.

Brayden, looking at Rick, "I'm going to stay here and keep the fire going."

Jordan and Pete both grab Rick by the arms. "We won't be long," and they walk off with him.

They take Rick out of the cameras' view and set him down on the ground. Pete gets down on his knees and looks Rick in the eyes. "You are dealing with powers far more imaginable than you can ever think. As you have found out, Jordan can control every part of your body. We can, let's say fry anything that you own, as you have found out. Jordan is going to take you home and we have decided to not erase your memory so you will remember everything that happened to you today."

Jordan is standing there listening to everything that Pete is telling Rick. He will have his say in a few minutes.

Pete stands and looks at Jordan. "I hope that I didn't overstep your boundaries."

Jordan smiles, "no, Pete, you did good. Now it's my turn." He looks down at Rick as he is sitting there looking up at him. "My UFO is waiting for us," he teleports Rick up to the Explorer. Jordan looks at Pete, "I'll be back in a little while." Then he teleports up into the Explorer.

Rick is now realizing that he has stepped way out of his league. With wide open eyes, he stands there watching Jordan appear next to him.

Jordan puts his hand on Rick's shoulder and pushes him down into a seat. He moves over and takes his seat at the controls. "Well, Rick I'm going to allow you to speak again."

Rick looks at Jordan, "what can I say?"

"Nothing, Rick, nothing. You have caused me enough problems with your arrogant behavior. I could completely erase your memory of today right now. But I'm not going to. I want you to remember who and what you are dealing with. If you are thinking that I can't erase your memory, I'll show you what I can do."

Rick's eyes go dark, "no, I believe you. I won't say anything. Give me my sight back, please, please."

Jordan restores Rick's sight, "okay Rick, I'll take you home now, and you know nothing."

Rick looks at Jordan as feels like he wants to start shaking from fear, "I know nothing."

Jordan takes Rick to a park about three miles from his home, "here you go, Rick. For your sake, I don't want to see or hear from you again." Jordan teleports Rick down into the park.

Rick realizes that he is on the ground and now can move his arms and legs. He looks around to see that he is the only one there. Then he figures out where he is, *I'm in the central park. I'm miles from home.* He looks down to see that he is still wearing the dress. He pulls it up to see that he doesn't have his pants on. He has to wear the dress all the way home. He starts walking home trying not to be seen, then a car goes by. He hears, "Hi, baby, what you doing tonight?" as a car load of teen-age boys drive by laughing at him.

Rick is walking home thinking about everything that happened to him today. It's been quite a terrible experience and something that he most likely will never forget. He has gained a lot of respect and fear of the ability that Jordan has. Although having to walk a few miles in a woman's dress isn't making him too happy.

He finally reaches his home just to find out that the door is locked and his keys are inside. Here he is standing there in front of his place in a dress. He walks around to the back of the house; he thinks that his bedroom window might be open. He looks at the window and it is open like he thought. The only problem is that it's too high for him to just crawl in. Now he is thinking, *daggone it, now I have to get a ladder from someone.* He thinks for a while, then heads over to the neighbor's house and knocks on the door. The neighbor opens the door and after seeing Rick standing there pops a big smile. "Must have been a great party," he says, as he looks Rick over. "I really like the hat."

Rick thinks for a second, he had forgotten about the hat. He just wanted to get home and cover up under a blanket. "Yes, it was. I locked my keys in the house. May I borrow your ladder so I can get into the back window?" he asks, as he is feeling stupid.

"Sure, it's in my shed. I'll get it for you." He takes a second look at Rick as he is going to the shed. He gets his ladder out for Rick. "When you are done, just bring it back and put it by the shed. I'll put it away later." He smiles as he hands the ladder to Rick. "You might want to consider taking the big hat off. I don't know if it will fit into your window." He starts to laugh as he walks back to his house.

Rick takes the ladder to the back of his house and puts it up by the window. He climbs up the ladder and throws the hat in the window, then works his way through the window and into his bedroom.

He changes into a pair of jeans and a t-shirt. Then he heads out to take the ladder back to the neighbor.

Brayden looks at Jordan, "I still have Rick's clothes."

"He only had a pair of sweatpants and a t-shirt on. I don't care what you do with them," Jordan replies.

Pete looks at Brayden, "go get them; I'll take care of them for you."

Brayden gets up from his seat, then heads over by the tent and picks up Rick's clothes.

Pete grins, "bring them over here" and he holds his hand out.

Brayden comes back and hands the clothes to Pete. Pete stands with Rick's clothes and throws them into the fire. "There that will take care of them."

Brayden laughs and sits back down in his camp chair. "I thought that was what you were going to do."

Jordan watches the clothes burn up and smiles, "I don't think that we will see him around here again. I scared the dickens out of him." He turns to Brayden, "I didn't tell you. I dropped him off a few miles away from his house." Jordan chuckles, "he had to walk all the way home in the dress that you put on him."

They start talking about Brayden's plan and how much fun they had acting their way through it. The cameras had run their batteries out, and now they could enjoy the rest of the camping weekend.

Cameras

They had a great time talking about how Jordan and Brayden came into the Knowing. Pete is especially happy that Jordan and he can be brothers. He has been waiting for a long time to be able to spend some time with Jordan. Now, Brayden on the other hand, is fun to be around.

Sunday they take the camping equipment down and put it away. Jordan has his Explorer ready to give Brayden a ride as he takes Pete back to the main ship. After dropping Pete off, they hover around the beaches, then head back to the campsite. With the campsite cleaned up, they head down to the house; where Brayden hops on his bike and heads home.

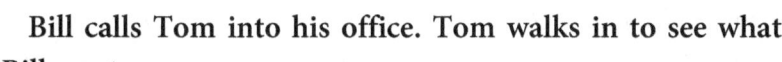

Bill calls Tom into his office. Tom walks in to see what Bill wants.

"Hi, Tom, we need to retrieve the cameras. I don't think that you will be spotted up at the campsite if you head there early in the morning." Bill tells him.

Tom looks at his watch, "okay, I'll pick them up around 6:30 tomorrow morning."

"Perfect, I can't wait to see what we have. I'll get in touch with Rick and see if he can be here to see what we have."

"Okay, I'll see you in the morning," and Tom walks out.

Bill gets on the phone and calls Rick.

Rick's phone rings, he answers, "hello."

"Hi, Rick, it's Bill. Do you have tomorrow morning off?"

Rick now thinks, *oh no! They're going to get the camera and what am I going to do?* "No, I have to work all day tomorrow," he says, trying to make an excuse. There is no way in heck he wants to be around when they see the videos.

"Oh darn, we were hoping that you could be here to see what we captured on the cameras," says Bill.

Rick acts disappointed, "darn; me, too."

"I'll give you a call tomorrow afternoon with a report on what we have," Bill tells him.

Rick gives a short reply, "okay."

"Talk to you tomorrow," Bill responds and hangs up the phone.

Rick slams his phone down thinking, *now what am I going to do? Those Aliens got me good! I've been had and had good! Now Bill and the whole world are going to see me and think that I was drunker than a skunk.* He kicks the coffee table. *And they put me in that stupid dress and put that big pink hat on me. I went to school with Jordan, and he's an Alien! They're everywhere; maybe even that Brayden is one. Jordan has powers that are unbelievable.* He sits there on the couch remembering what Jordan did to him; then he falls asleep on the couch.

Tom comes walking into the headquarters with a plastic bag in his hand. Bill is standing there with the morning coffee talking with a couple other members.

"Good, you have the cameras. We were talking about them and can't wait to see what they have on them," Bill says, as Tom hands the bag to him.

"Come on guys, let's see what we have. Rick promised me that the Aliens visited that area frequently." They all head into the conference room where they have a computer hooked up to video projector so they all can view pictures on a large screen on the wall.

Bill hands the bag of cameras back to Tom, "you know which one will have the best view."

Tom takes the cameras out of the bag and places them on the table. He looks them over, "okay here it is; number one. I believe that this one will be the first to look at." He hands it to Bill.

In the meantime, Bill is turning on the computer and the video projector. He takes the camera from Tom then plugs a jumper cord into it. Then he plugs the cord into the USB port in the computer. Tom turns off the lights as the video starts. The room is quiet until the video starts; then all of a sudden there was a loud gasping sound then a loud, "wow!"

Bill stops the video, and looks at the others in the room, "Rick was right, we have a UFO."

"Play it again," says Tom.

Bill sets the video back to start. He clicks on play, and a UFO instantly appears, a hatch opens, and they can see

Jordan walk into the UFO. They look at the video in disbelief as it fades out of view.

Bill reverses the video to the point where Jordan is walking into the UFO. He stops it and freezes it so he can print out a picture. He stops the video and unplugs the camera and puts the others into the bag that Tom had them in.

"I have to find Rick and congratulate him." He says as he turns the conference room light on.

Bill takes the cameras and puts them in his desk drawer. He walks over to the printer and picks up the picture and turns to the others. "I'm going to see Rick and show him what we found. We'll talk about how we are going to handle this discovery later. For now, let's keep it to ourselves."

They agree, as Bill heads out the door. Bill, being excited, rushes to his car and drives to Home Depot where Rick works. He parks his car and walks into the store. He walks up to the first employee that he finds. "Can you tell me where I can find Rick Peterson?"

"I think he works in hardware; you'll be able to find him there."

Bill walks to the hardware department and finds an employee. "Hi, I'm looking for Rick Peterson."

The employee turns to Bill, "he isn't working today; he will be here tomorrow. Is there anything that I can help you with?"

"No, thank you. I'll talk to him tomorrow," Bill says trying to be polite. He turns around and walks back to his car.

Rick is reading one of his photography magazines and hears a knock on his door. He gets up and walks over and opens the door to see Bill standing there with a big smile. Not wanting to waste any time, he walks in. Rick is now thinking, *oh no, I've been had, here it comes.*

Bill hands Rick the picture of the UFO, "we got them, Rick, we got them," he says with excitement in his eyes.

Rick looks at the picture and can't believe it. Now he really doesn't know what to do. If he gets involved with the discovery, he knows Jordan is going to get him. Rick's payday is a thing of the past. Now saving himself from the wrath of the Aliens is all that he cares about. He looks at Bill, "you got them." He hands the picture back to Bill, "now it is yours. I have done my part, and I'm done with everything."

"Yes, Rick, but you reported it to us. Don't you want the credit? We now have proof that Aliens are here. We had five cameras out there, and I bet all five have the UFO from different perspectives." Bill looks at Rick, "we got them, you and I. Just imagine what the news is going to do with this."

Rick is thinking, *dang I'm not going to be famous! I have to get out of this; I can't take the chance.*

"No, Bill, I gave you the information. Now, please keep me out of any part of it," Rick tells Bill as he is remembering Jordan's powers. "I'll be watching for it on the news; that will be good enough for me."

Bill looks at Rick, "I can understand that limelight can be a bit too much for some people. I'll be thinking about you,

Rick; this will most likely be the last time that we meet."
Bill reaches out to shake Rick's hand.

Rick shakes his hand and Bill walks to the door, opens it
and leaves.

Rick picks up his magazine and tosses it across the room
in anger thinking, *they got me. I know that they are here
and I found them. Now I can't get any credit for the
discovery. I get nothing but a wrecked car.*

Final check

Jordan finishes his breakfast and is thinking about going up to the camping area. He wants to check to see if the cameras are still there. He has the feeling that they have been removed. Jordan receives a message, *good morning, Jordan, I was listening to your thoughts. I did some checking and you had a visitor in your camping area. The cameras have been removed.*

Jordan replies with a message, *thanks, Tarke.*

Tarke messages back, *you have a big problem with the cameras. You removed the memory cards and had Harec cleaned them for you. We have found out that they have extra memory. The cameras have a factory installed ten-minute memory, and they have the Explorer and you on video.*

Jordan replies, "*I'll see you in a few minutes. I would like to have Karen, Pete, and Harec available. I have business that I need to take care of immediately.*

Tarke replies, *they will be waiting for you.*

Jordan messages Harec, *hi Harec, I need your memory removal skills. Tarke will fill you in on what is going on. I'll see you in a few minutes.*

Jordan knows that time is his first priority. He looks at his mother who is sitting at the kitchen table with him. He puts his dishes in the sink quickly and turns to Mother, "I have urgent business and have to leave. Love you. I'll tell you about it later." He rushes out of the house and to the backyard where he has his Explorer waiting.

Jordan's mother is wondering what is going on as she is looking out the back window watching Jordan leave. All of a sudden the Explorer appears, Jordan runs in and the Explorer fades out of sight. She stands there thinking that whatever it is, it must be important.

In only a couple minutes Jordan is on the ship and heading to Tarke's office. He walks into Tarke's office to see Karen, Pete, and Harec standing there with Tarke.

Tarke looks at Jordan, "I have told them what is going on and gave them your plans."

Jordan grins as he knows that he and Tarke can read each other's thoughts and knows what he is going to do. He looks at them, "come with me, I have my Explorer waiting for us." They rush out to the bridge for the Explorer. Some of the crew members watch them rushing by as they wonder what they are doing.

They get into the Explorer and Jordan leaves for the UFO reporting organization's building in Spring Lake, Michigan. Jordan hovers over the organization's building, "I think it is going to be best if we use the area behind the building."

Jordan puts the Explorer in hold mode and looks over at Karen, Pete, and Harec. "You have your jobs, let's get this done."

Jordan looks over at Pete knowing what he is thinking. "Yes, Brother, you can. Harec, will you please take care of Pete's job, also?"

Harec replies, "no problem."

Jordan looks at them, "okay, I'll let you know when it's safe for you."

"Remember, Jordan, ten feet is the range of your transmitter," Harec tells Jordan.

Jordan grins and teleports down to the back of the organization's building. He starts walking around to the front, as Karen and Harec teleport down.

Jordan stands at the door for a second thinking about how he has to handle this situation. He opens the door and walks in. Tom is sitting at the front desk looking at him in amazement, knowing who Jordan is from the video. "Can I help you?" he asks.

Jordan smiles, "yes, I would like to see Bill."

Bill is in the conference room with a couple other members talking about the video.

Tom, looking at Jordan, "yes, I'll get him." He gets up and rushes to the conference room. "Bill, you will never guess who is here asking for you. It's that guy that got into the UFO!"

Bill turns, "really."

Tom replies, "yes, really. He is out by the front desk."

Bill calmly walks out to the front desk to see Jordan standing there. "Hi, Jordan, what brings you here today?"

Jordan looks at Bill and Tom. "This is the UFO reporting organization, isn't it? I have something that I would like to talk to everybody about."

Jordan is tuned into Bill's thinking and smiles. He knows that Bill is jumping for joy thinking that he is going to get the whole story. "Why, sure; everybody is in the conference room. Come on, Tom, you should be with us also." Bill points the way, "come with us this way."

They walk into the conference room with Jordan. As everyone is staring at him, Jordan smiles and sits down at the first seat that he sees. Bill is now thinking, he is sitting; this is going to be good.

Jordan, knowing how to run a meeting and wanting everyone seated, stands. "I have some things that I need to tell you." Trying to get their full attention, "Bill, please take a seat," he holds in a smile; Bill sits down.

Jordan says to himself, I have them where I want them. He starts walking around the table. "You are a dedicated group and are looking for proof of alien life." He has their full attention as he is walking around the conference room table. "You are wondering why I am here. That is something that you will never know. You think that I'm an Alien and you saw me and a UFO."

Jordan stops at the end of the table and looks at them. "And you will never know."

Jordan steps back and messages Karen. *Come on in I have them all in suspension. It just took a quick walk around the table.*

Karen and Harec come in the front door. Jordan walks out of the conference room to meet them. "Finding the cameras wasn't hard, they have them in the conference room. I spotted them as soon as I entered."

"That makes our job easier," Karen says with a smile.

They head into the conference room where five people are sitting there in a daze.

"There they are," says Jordan as he points at them.

Karen moves them over where she can remove the memory cards. She lines the cameras up and takes the cards out and sets them next to the camera. "Your turn, Harec."

Harec picks up each camera and waves the disabler over it. "That will erase the internal memory." He looks over at the computer. "I don't know what they have on their hard drive, but that is about to also be gone, just in case they copied any video."

Jordan looks around and doesn't spot the picture that Bill is supposed to have. "I'm going to look around for Bill's picture of me."

Jordan walks out and into each office room. It didn't take long when he spotted the picture on Bill's desk. He picks up the picture and folds it and puts it in his pocket.

Pete, in Jordan's Explorer, hovers directly over Rick's home. He puts the Explorer into hold and thinks, *well, Rick, it's my turn now. Here I come.* Pete teleports into Rick's living room.

Rick jumps up from his seat on the couch. "I didn't do anything. I haven't told anyone anything", he says in panic, suddenly seeing Pete standing there.

Pete doesn't have the ability to do what Jordan can, but pure intimidating power is on his side. He looks at Rick, "come over here," Pete says forcefully.

Rick knowing what Jordan can do, doesn't hesitate to walk over to Pete. "Good boy," Pete says, holding a smile back. "You and I are going to take a nice ride just because I like you."

Rick, now half petrified, nods his head in an okay motion. Pete teleports Rick up to the Explorer, then quickly teleports himself up. Pete appears in the Explorer alongside Rick. He puts his hand on Rick's shoulder and smiles, "have a seat."

Rick sits down with a puzzled look thinking, *what is he going to do? Where, are we going?*

Pete takes control of the Explorer and heads back to see Jordan. He stops in the same place behind the UFO organization's building. Rick is sitting there in total amazement with what just happened. This is the second time that he has been in a UFO.

"Okay, Rick, you and I are going to take a little walk," Pete says as he puts the Explorer in hold mode.

Pete decides that it will be better if he teleports down with Rick this time. He smiles at Rick, then puts his arm around him and they teleport down behind the building.

Rick is now standing there in a daze. This is almost too much to handle for him.

Pete, with his hand on Rick's arm, walks him to the front of the building. Rick looks up at the building knowing where he is. Now he is totally blank about what is going on. Pete messages Jordan, *we are coming in.*

Jordan messages a reply, *come on in, we are waiting for you.*

Pete opens the door, "you first," he says with a big smile. They both walk in to see Karen, Harec, and Jordan standing by the front desk.

"Hi, Pete, you brought a friend with you, " says Jordan knowing what is next.

Rick stands there now thinking that this isn't going to be good.

Jordan, knowing that Rick is not under any of their powers, does the same as Pete, intimidation. "Follow me, Rick," and they head to the conference room. Rick looks in to see five people sitting there with blank faces. He looks at Jordan in fear of what he is seeing.

Jordan can't punish Rick anymore and immediately puts Rick into suspension like the others. Karen takes Rick and sits him down in a chair.

"Well, we have everything ready. We were just waiting for you to bring the star of the show," Jordan says with a smile as he is looking at Pete. "Harec has reset their brains to thinking that this is the first time that they will see the video."

Pete looks at the doorway to see Tom standing there. "I was wondering about why you had him there."

Harec replies, "when we leave, I'll trigger their brains to start and he will turn off the lights like normal."

Pete smiles, "I wish that I could see what is going to happen."

Jordan puts his arm around Pete, "you will. Harec took care of that for us. Let's go and let the show begin." And they all walk out and around back to the Explorer.

The video

Two days later Brayden comes over to see Jordan.

"Hi, Jordan, what do you want?" Brayden asks.

"You are going to have your first learning session today, so we'll have to go to the main ship," answers Jordan.

Brayden looking at Jordan with a big smile, "let's go; I can't wait." He starts heading out of the house.

Jordan grins and waves goodbye to his mother, as he catches up with Brayden. "I guess you are a little anxious," he says with a smile.

They head up to the camping area with Jordan trying to keep up with Brayden. Jordan is having fun with Brayden's excitement; not telling him that they could have left from his backyard. They get up to the camp area and Jordan has his Explorer there ready for them. It didn't take long and they were heading into Harec's med room, where Harec is waiting for Brayden.

Jordan smiles, "he's ready, he almost had me on a dead run getting here." Jordan looks at Brayden, "I'll most likely be in Tarke's office. I'll meet you there," and Jordan walks out leaving Harec to handle Brayden.

Jordan is on his way to see Tarke when one of the crew members stops him. "Hi, Jordan, you left here the other day in a big hurry," he says in a questioning mood.

Jordan smiles, not needing to keep it secret. "Yes, I have been having a problem with someone trying to find out,"

Jordan looks at the crew member with a grin, "if we are real."

"Just wondering. I've been too busy to ask anyone. I'm sure you have it taken care of."

"Yes, we do," Jordan replies.

"Thanks for letting me know; have a great day," and the crew member walks off.

Jordan walks into Tarke's office, "good morning, Tarke. I brought Brayden in for his first learning experience," Jordan tells Tarke as he takes a seat.

Tarke looks up from his screen, "I noticed he was a little excited," he says with a smile. "Harec and Brayden are going to meet us in the conference room in a couple minutes."

"Oh, okay," Jordan replies as he stands up from his seat.

They both walk out and to the conference room. When they enter, there sits Brayden in the middle of asking Harec questions about everything that he learned. Tarke and Jordan take their seats. The only one who noticed them is Harec with a big smile.

Jordan reaches over and gives Brayden a small push on his shoulder, "slow down, let everything settle down. You won't need to ask so many questions."

Brayden turns to Jordan, "when did you get here?"

Jordan smiles, "Tarke and I walked in with you."

Harec and Tarke chuckle, then Tarke turns to Harec. "You have some information for them, don't you?"

Harec looks at Jordan, "I sure do."

Tarke smiles, "I do know that you two are going to enjoy this. I have seen it."

Harec points at the room wall and a video starts showing.

"Brayden, it's a video of my visit to the UFO organization that I told you about."

The video starts as Tom turns off the lights in their conference room. Tom takes a seat next to Bill and Rick.

Brayden laughs loudly, "you didn't tell me that Rick was there."

"That was Pete's last minute idea and I couldn't refuse him."

"I bet he was sitting there madder than a wet hen!" says Brayden, as he is calming his laughter down.

The video continues. They watch as Pete and Brayden set up the camp. The UFO group is commenting on how good the video is from the small spy cameras. Tom is getting credit for hiding them so well. They see Jordan come into view. Bill comments that Jordan is one of the suspected Alien's friends. He also mentions that one of the other two is supposed to be an Alien, but he doesn't know which one. He turns to Rick, "you know, Rick. Which one is that Alien?"

Rick is now extremely upset being placed in this predicament and figures what the heck. "That tall older one on the left, I think," he points out Pete.

In the discussion, Brayden walks out of view. They are now talking about Pete and that he doesn't look like any type of Alien that they would imagine. Brayden comes walking into view with Rick. Bill looks at the video then back at Rick, "that's you?"

Tom points at the video, "stop it. Put it on pause."

Bill puts the video on pause. They study the video picture, then Bill looks at Rick, "what the heck are you wearing?"

Rick is embarrassed and has nothing more to say to them. He just looks down at his feet.

One of the other members in the room says, "the big pink hat really sets his dress off."

Bill presses play for the video. They sit back and listen to Brayden, Pete and Jordan talk.

Bill looks at Rick, "so you are quite a drinker."

Tom points out all the beer cans that they found in the woods.

One of the UFO investigators stands and points at the screen. "There is Rick's Alien!" he is pointing at Brayden in his green wetsuit and Alien mask. He laughs and points at Rick, "you caught yourself, a drunk and his lies."

Bill stops the video and walks over to turn the lights on. Rick is speechless sitting there looking at his feet.

"Rick, I thought you were credible. You cost us a lot of money and time. And our payoff is to see you in a prom dress and a pink hat. And to top it off, you are sitting with your friends in that getup, drunk. Then you accuse them of being Aliens. I wouldn't doubt it if they never talk to you again."

Bill turns to Tom, "get him out of here."

Tom shows Rick the door and closes it after he walks out.

The video stops; Brayden looks at Jordan, "we got him."

The story continues

Special thanks to those who have inspired me to continue writing until this book was finished, and helped me through editing and getting it to publishing.

My wife Laurie, for her patience and ideas.

My good friend Betty Clark for her editing help.

My Facebook - "Author Lon Hieftje" friends for your support.

During the process of writing this sequel book #2 "Jordan Kingston – Keeping the Secret." Thanks for following Jordan and Brayden as they explored their new-found knowledge. Now that you know Jordan and Brayden, you don't want to miss their new adventures in book #3 Jordan Kingston Adventures.

This is my second book did you like it?

Thank you for purchasing Jordan Kingston Keeping the secret.

I spent over a year writing "Jordan's" first book. By the end of the book, I ended up with a new friend in Jordan. I hope Jordan became a friend of yours, also. I haven't forgotten Brayden; he is a cool kid and a fun friend to be around. They both have been telling me about their continuing adventures for the next book. Their next book – wow- you won't believe their stories, or will you?

Please visit my website www.lonspress.com and write a short review. It is always nice to read my readers thoughts.

Thank You

Lon Hieftje

www.ingramcontent.com/pod-product-compliance
Lightning Source LLC
Chambersburg PA
CBHW072219170626
46813CB00003B/1004